JAGGER

Julius Falconer

PNEUMA SPRINGS PUBLISHING UK

First Published in 2010 by:
Pneuma Springs Publishing

Jagger

ISBN: 978-1-905809-99-8

This is a work of fiction. Names, characters, places and incidents are either products of the author's imagination or are used fictitiously. Any resemblance to actual events or locales or persons, living or dead, save those clearly in the public domain, is purely coincidental.

Pneuma Springs Publishing
A Subsidiary of Pneuma Springs Ltd.
7 Groveherst Road, Dartford Kent, DA1 5JD.
E: admin@pneumasprings.co.uk
W: www.pneumasprings.co.uk

A catalogue record for this book is available from the British Library.

JAGGER

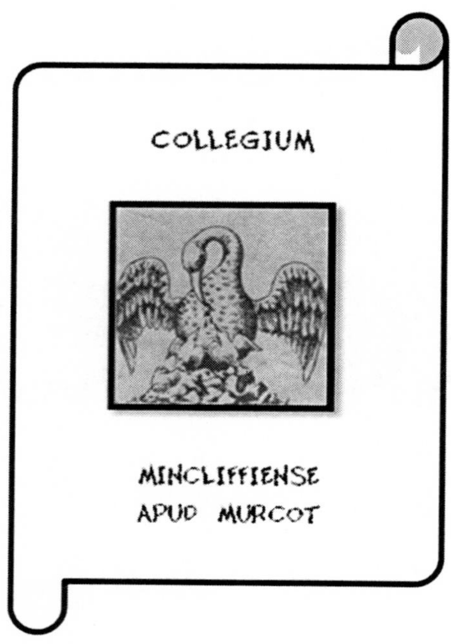

In memory of my much loved and respected parents

Aileen Norma
(1912-1993)
and
Richard Lionel
(1908-2005)

who sent me to 'Mincliffe College'

PROLEGOMENON

'Have you ever killed a man?' Jagger asked his companion.

'No, of course not. Why, have you?' Crudson replied with a question of his own.

'Yes, I'm afraid I have.'

'Are you going to tell me about it, or was that not the purpose of your question?'

'Yes, I think I'd like to tell you – if you've the time to listen.'

The two men were seated in easy chairs in front of a log fire on a cold winter's evening. While the snow-storm raged outside, all within was quiet, except for the stately tick-tock of the nineteenth-century French long-case clock that stood in the corner (made by Le Couvé in Napoléonville to celebrate the events of 24 February 1848 – although its present owner had never been able to confirm the clockmaker's identity or location with other information). The friends each held a glass of golden cognac, which they sipped with appreciation, knowledgeably. Cigar smoke wound up to the ceiling. It was precisely the right place and moment for a story.

'It happened a few years ago now, in Coventry. I was then an actor with the rep there, as you'll remember, and we were doing O'Neill's *The Iceman Cometh* – pretty ambitious, you might say: but then it was still early days at the new – well, newish – theatre, and the management were trying out what worked and what didn't. Also in the cast was a chap called Higgins, Ed Higgins, whom I had disliked on sight. Why? I don't know. Was it his gloomy face, sullen frown and big ears? Or his spiky hair and restless hands? Or the misanthropy lurking in his porcine eyes? Heaven knows. Anyway, we never seemed to get on, although as members of the same cast we inevitably saw quite a bit of each other. The part of Margie was being taken by a girl called Amy, new to the company, and she was good, no doubt about it. Whether she'd ever been a prostitute in real life and could play her part from experience, I've no idea: I was too gentlemanly to ask. She had a good figure, an effective brassy voice and a mobile face which enabled her to put on a huge variety of expressions: surprise, hate, dejection, anticipation, knowingness, boredom – you name it. What she saw in Higgins I've no idea. He was, as far as I could see, an overweight, self-indulgent, spendthrift boor, although he could act, I'll give him that. It fell out that Higgins and Amy seemed attracted to each other. The chemistry of affection will always be a mystery to me, and I don't suppose anyone will ever fathom it. Where Higgins was morose, and ugly with it, she was vivacious and *very* pretty: prettier than almost anybody else I've ever seen. Where he was heavy and lumbering, in both physique and manner, she was slim and animated. Soon their mutual attachment made itself known to the rest of us, and most, I suppose, took it in their stride. There is, after all, nothing exceptional in a young – well, youngish - man and a young woman, thrown together in the way of their profession, making a go of it.

'However, one of our number took great exception to their friendship. This was a bloke called Prosser, who played the part of McGloin, the ex-policeman. Ned Prosser was in his fifties, old enough to be Amy's father, but he fancied himself a bit as a magnet for females. The fact that he'd already divorced two wives didn't seem to strike him as working against this flattering self-image of his. If two women got close enough to marry him and then decided they'd made a bad bargain, you'd think the penny would drop, but it doesn't seem to have done so. Prosser began to demonstrate his jealousy of Higgins, first of all, with derogatory and insulting remarks to his face, then with more general comments to the company at large, until it all got a bit of an embarrassment and, to be honest, a bit of a bore. In a repertory company, with however many extras, a stupid feud is not just a nuisance: it's unsettling. The director had a word with Prosser; so did the manager; but neither seemed to do much good, except temporarily.

'Eventually the manager told Prosser that he'd have either to master his dislike of Higgins or to quit the company. Things calmed down a bit with this ultimatum. You know those two bits, one in Act II and one in Act IV, when McGloin and Mosher square up to each other? Mosher's a one-time circus artiste. The first time, Rocky and Chuck dive in between them to prevent fisticuffs; the second time, it's Rocky alone who prevents further trouble. The scenes took on such realism that the cast were increasingly worried that a sort of *I Pagliacci* dénouement would take place before their very eyes. And talk about exciting the audience!

'Well, one day Higgins took Amy out to lunch at a café in Hertford Street. Prosser followed them. They had not long begun their meal, when Prosser came up to their table and started a scene. First of all he told Higgins that he was nothing but a "cockered earth-vexing pignut" – Shakespeare! – a lousy actor, a fat, ugly peasant, a blot on the landscape and I don't know what else besides. He didn't shout but spat his words out. Then he flourished a fist and threatened Higgins with violence if he didn't leave Amy alone. And then – and this, of course, riled Higgins more than anything – he laid a hand on Amy's arm and said something like, "Come on, love, you'd be much better off with me". Well, Higgins jumped up and pushed Prosser in the chest, hard. Prosser lost his balance and fell on to the table behind him, breaking it, before leaping to his feet and making for Higgins. Higgins was ready, and in seconds a fight was in progress round the café. At the first sign of trouble, the café owner had phoned the police, and within a few minutes a couple of constables arrived to put an end to it all. Witnesses testified that Prosser was the aggressor, but because Higgins wasn't willing to press charges, Prosser got away with a caution and paying for the damage. As soon as news got back to the theatre, the manager sacked Prosser and told him to go away and find something to do that would enable him to get over his feelings.

'Prosser had no choice, particularly as Higgins had treated him with something approaching generosity, perhaps unexpected in such a lumbering, clumsy oaf, and of course the police had cautioned him as well. Prosser left, and that was the last we saw of him – for a time. I heard later that he was out of work for some months and then got a job at Nottingham rep. The Belgrade manager must have said in his reference that Prosser wasn't normally a troublemaker.

'Prosser, however, hadn't finished with his attempt to wheedle Amy away from Higgins. About six months after his dismissal, he reappeared in Coventry and asked for his old job back. The manager naturally refused. Prosser hung around Amy's lodgings, accosting her on her way to the theatre, attending performances and applauding excessively – we were then playing *Arsenic and Old Lace*, and Amy was, of course, Elaine - sending up messages to meet her after the show. Eventually the manager told the police, and they warned him off. He disappeared again.

'In due course, Higgins and Amy got married. Although I still thought Higgins a quite intolerable lout, I admit that Amy did induce in him a slight improvement. He lost weight, shaved more often, became slightly more civilised. They bought a small terraced house in Queensland Avenue off Hearsall Common and settled down to the tedious life of repertory actors: new parts to master, endless rehearsals, performance after performance, no social life to speak of. Every so often one of them would be laid off temporarily, and it was more likely to be Higgins, as the management recognised that Amy was a popular figure. Not many plays call for a hulking brute, however theatrically talented.

'It all came to a head when they'd been married about a year. I think they were happy enough, in so far as happiness is possible in this vale of tears - or, as Shakespeare has it, this world of vile ill-favour'd faults. Prosser suddenly appeared out of nowhere. He was raddled: blear-eyed from drink, paunchy from lack of exercise, stupid from unemployment. He looked as if he were sleeping on the streets, which I daresay he was. It's sad to see a man let himself go, even, or perhaps particularly, one so unattractive as Prosser, and to embark on the decline from which salvation is so difficult. He had clearly been lurking about the theatre, waiting for an opportunity to accost Higgins, and his vigil paid off one night as his quarry left the theatre alone after a performance. Prosser followed Higgins as far as Spon End – a quieter part of town than Corporation Street! - where he grabbed him by the shoulder, spun him round and challenged him. Either he gave up Amy or he, Prosser, would kill him there and then. Now Prosser had run to seed: he was flabby and half-drunk to boot, but the anger in his eyes testified to his determination. At one time he must have been a powerful man. Higgins was younger than his adversary and no weakling, as I've tried to convey to you, but he too was decayed, and the result of a fight between the two men wasn't easy to predict. Anyway, they set to, and it became clear that a death would be the end, nothing less. In height and weight the men were matched. In experience? I don't know. Fists were flailing. Higgins, the victim, wore only shoes, whereas Prosser, the aggressor, had, perhaps deliberately, donned boots, and he used them. The two men swayed about in the street, swapping punches in a silence studded by panting, kicks and blows. Higgins fell and struck his head on a projecting doorstep and lay still, blood seeping from the wound. Prosser kicked him, laughed and lurched away, back towards the centre of town.'

'Hold on,' Crudson said, 'I thought you were going to tell me how *you* killed a man.'

'I was, and I am,' the other replied. 'You see, Higgins wasn't dead: stunned, momentarily unconscious, yes, but not dead. After a few minutes, he stirred and made as if to get up off the pavement. His hand went to his head and came away bloodied. It was at that moment that I stepped in.'

'You? What do you mean?'

'I'd followed the men from the theatre. I'd come out just after Higgins, and I saw Prosser step out of the shadows and set off behind him. I guessed that no good could come of the encounter. I'd followed the affair from the beginning, remember, and I was intrigued. That's morbid, perhaps, but it's also human nature. "Sweep on, you fat and greasy citizens," I thought to myself and determined to be in at the kill, whichever way it went. I watched the fight from a distance, and as soon as Prosser had moved off a safe distance – safe for me, I mean – I approached the stricken actor. I looked quickly up and down the street, checking that no one was about, and then I grasped Higgins by the hair of his head and brought his head hard down on the edge of the stone step. The *coup de grâce*.'

'What?' Crudson cried out in his horror. 'But that's murder, cold-bloodied murder!'

'Well, aren't you going to ask me why?'

'That's horrible: what on earth possessed you?'

'Love,' Jagger said simply.

'Love?'

'Yes, love for Amy. You see, I'd set my heart on Amy from the beginning: a quite fabulous creature.'

'Why didn't you say something?'

'Higgins got in before me, and I was no match for him. At that stage I respected Amy and her choice: it was not my business to prise the two apart, or even to attempt to do so; but I hoped that my time would come. Gradually, my regard for Amy turned to love and then to passion and finally to obsession. I could hardly wait to see the end of Higgins and then to stake my claim.'

'But would Amy have had you?'

'I don't know, do I? But I reckoned I stood a chance, perhaps better than anyone else in the cast, anyway. When I saw Higgins at my mercy, I took a split-second decision and dispatched him. He would probably not have survived Prosser's beating, anyway, so I was only helping him on his way, putting him out of his misery, if you like. Do you know that scene in Remarque's *All Quiet on the Western Front*, about – or perhaps I should say against - the first world war? The narrator comes across a comrade too badly wounded to survive more than a few days and, although at the moment beyond pain, already close to dying in agony. One of his companions whispers, "Shouldn't we just take a revolver and put an end to it?" They don't – at least that's the impression the text gives – but reading that emotional passage, I wonder how I should have reacted in similar circumstances. Now I know. Does that make me a heartless criminal? Maybe it does.'

'What happened next?' Crudson asked in disbelief.

'I went to a public phone-box and phoned the police. I didn't give a name. I just said that I'd witnessed a fight, that the victim was obviously dead, and that the killer was even then walking along Spon Street towards the centre of town. I described him and then hung up.'

'And?'

'Well, he was tried – admitted the murder quite happily, even eagerly – and was sent down for life.'

'Go on,' Crudson said reluctantly, wanting, despite himself, to hear the end of the story.

'Well, after a suitable period – I didn't want any suspicions floating to the surface - I approached Amy and told her of my love for her.' He smiled as he said this, but it was a bitter smile.

'You mean obsession. What did she say?'

'She said she didn't love me. I asked her whether she had found anyone else. No, she hadn't, she had no thoughts of another man, let alone remarriage. She was going to stay on her own and try to come to terms with her loss. Well, I understood that, of course: "Some griefs are medicinable" as the Bard has it, and I was prepared to wait, now that I knew I could dream on in hope.' He paused to take up another cigar and light it. There was a deep silence in the room, punctuated only by the grandfather clock marking the steady march of time. Crudson spoke again after a few minutes.

'Why have you told me this?' he asked. 'I thought I was going to get a story of derring-do, of heroism, of the intrepid rescue of a damsel in distress, perhaps.'

'That's what I gave you,' Jagger said. 'I rescued Amy from an unsuitable husband.'

'But you said that Amy and Higgins seemed happy in their marriage.'

'Maybe I did, and it's true, but for all that Higgins wasn't fit for anything. It's just that Amy couldn't see it. I released her from a relationship that could never have brought her happiness in the long run.'

'That's the height of arrogance!' Crudson exclaimed.

'No, I don't think so: it's the balanced assessment of a scholar and - in my own way - a mystic.'

'Hell, you're conceited; I despise you for it. But you still haven't told me your reasons for recounting your story tonight. Why take me into your confidence? I now wish you hadn't.'

'Do you? Well, I can hardly blame you. It's not a pretty story, but I don't really see that I acted unreasonably. People's emotions carry them away and make them do silly things, and tragedy is the result. I was merely a spectator of the follies of others, until, in the final act, I stepped in to right a wrong. There was a certain justice: Higgins died on the feast of St Edward the Martyr. On the other hand, my conscience troubles me ever so slightly, and I've appreciated this opportunity to get things off my chest. I'm sorry you've been cast in the role of father confessor, but I did ask you first, if you remember.'

'Right, well, as your father confessor, I think you should tell the police – and I'm serious.'

'What, after all this time?' exclaimed Jagger. 'What good would that do?'

'For a start it would get Prosser out of prison.'

''Fraid not. He didn't survive three months in prison: just sort of faded away.'

'Well, I'm sorry for that. Then it would establish the truth of the matter, once for all. "While you live, tell truth and shame the devil!"'

'Huh,' Jagger sneered. 'Who'd benefit from that? If you can quote Shakespeare, I can quote Voltaire: "There are truths which are not for all men or for all times". In other words, if I understand the great man correctly, there are some considerations more powerful than truth. What is truth, anyway? "Rarely pure and never simple," said Wilde. No, I shall keep my counsel, as I trust you will keep yours. There's nothing to be gained by raking over old embers.'

Jagger took several deep puffs at his cigar, seemingly untroubled in his mind, now that he had unburdened it. Time had worn on, and the night was considerably advanced. Crudson was unsure what to think. There was a certain justice in Jagger's view, but none the less it stuck in his craw. He thought he might sleep on it.

'Good night, Jagger,' he said, without warmth, as he rose from his chair.

'A night-cap?' the other queried.

'No, I think not,' he replied. 'We've probably talked enough for one evening – more than enough. See you in the morning – if the Lord spares us in our wickedness.'

One

First of all, dear reader, I had better tell you, since it will not be obvious from the printed page or, at this early stage, from the elegance and fluency of style, that your chronicler is Julius Falconer. You may wonder why I am bothering to tell you this: is the name not on the book's spine, the front cover and the title page? Is it not sufficiently obvious to all already? The truth is that Wickfield – Stan to his wife and to his one and only friend, if indeed he has that many, Wickfield to everybody else – has sometimes given you an account of his cases under cover of my name, on pretext that I am incapacitated or tired or away on holiday. This time, however, the boot is on the other foot: he has been ordered by his lawful superiors to take sabbatical leave, ostensibly to produce some document for the Home Office, but really, I am fairly certain, to brush up on his waning detective skills (victims of increasing years, you know). I am sure you are grateful for this small mercy of Providence, since you can now relax, in the knowledge that this story, of how Lionel Jagger came to be the victim of murder, is in safe hands. If I should start to wander into the byways of literature, philosophy, theology, history or music, which is Wickfield's constant gripe, be assured that it is always in the interests of your continued enjoyment. I should append here a final introductory comment: the following narrative is based entirely on the inspector's own handwritten account, judiciously pruned here and there (you will be glad to hear), smoothed out, corrected where necessary and rephrased with the urbanity and chic that is, ahem, my hallmark. You have before you, therefore, Wickfield content in Falconer garb: a marriage made in heaven and worth every penny of the purchase price.

Our story begins at Mincliffe College in the year of grace 1975. It is funny how things go, is it not? Wickfield and Spooner had no sooner wrapped up the dreadful business of the murder of Adrian Carrick at Grant School for Girls, seven miles away (a tale told in *Mr Carrick is Laid to Rest*), than they were called out to Mincliffe College for Boys a little later that same autumn. Not only that, but it was the second time they had had occasion to investigate dark misdeeds at Mincliffe: in July of the previous year, they had investigated the death of the unfortunate Charles Trevelyan in the case of *The Founder's Portrait*. It is true that on that occasion the college was only indirectly involved in the sequence of events; none the less, the inspector and his sergeant had had to spend quite a bit of time with staff, boys and parents. It was therefore with something approaching familiarity that the two detectives drove up the imposing drive that led to the college. If you do not know Mincliffe, let me just tell you that it is a mid-nineteenth-century pile, in Puginesque neo-Gothic, set in fifty acres of sports fields, woods and parkland, encumbered (not too strong a word) by twentieth-century additions (science laboratories, music rooms, Byzantinesque chapel, gymnasium etc). To find it, you will need to leave Evesham or Broadway on the A44, turn off on to a side-road south of the village of Wickhamford, proceed half-a-mile west until you come to the tiny hamlet of Murcot, where massive wrought-iron gates give access to Mincliffe territory. Proceed up the tree-lined drive and park by the circle of lawn that graces the frontage. You have arrived at Mincliffe College, Roman Catholic seat of learning and formative academy for generations of schoolboys, the vast majority of them, no doubt for their sins, boarders.

Hold on a minute! There's a curious arrow here: something like ↫. I think that must mean we're going back in time. I wish Wickfield's notes made a bit more sense! Right, all set: we've gone back a month or two. Here we go: precise time unspecified, but I think autumn of the year of grace 1974.

The best way to introduce you to some of the characters in the drama [he writes – I think] is perhaps to eavesdrop on a staff-room conversation that took place one day after lunch. You will appreciate that this scene owes its existence in great part to my, Falconer's, fertile imagination; the characters, however, if the inspector is to be trusted, are real enough. I should also add, to assuage your doubts, that, since the topic of conversation was rehearsed in one of the school magazines Wickfield apparently chanced to read in reception one day, his suggestion probably has a fringe of authenticity. (Was it not Thomas Aquinas who referred to animals, or at least some animals, as having a fringe of intelligence?) The participants, sitting round a coffee-table nursing mugs of hot beverage – tea or coffee, according to choice – were Fr Frank Hendon, the bursar; Fr Mike Bedford, the deputy head (or, in Mincliffe parlance, the vice-president); Helen Mansfield, teacher of biology and one of the few women on the staff; Lionel Jagger, head of English and drama; and Russell Smith, head of art. Mike Bedford was commenting on the boys' expectations of a university place.

'What worries me,' he was saying, 'is that the boys are often so complacent. They think it's enough to get decent grades at "A"-Level, and they'll sail into the university of their choice. It's not like that, and it's going to get worse.'

'So do we shake the boys out of their complacency,' asked Fr Hendon, 'or urge the government to see that more universities are built?'

'There's no point in building more universities, is there?' Miss Mansfield put in. 'Let's say that in the future everybody who wishes to attend university is guaranteed a place. What would be the result of that? Simply that, without any sense of competition, standards would inevitably fall. Nobody would try.'

'What you're suggesting, Helen,' Russell Smith chipped in, 'is that you engineer a system in which some would-be university candidates are deliberately excluded in order to keep standards up. Isn't that using people as a means to an end?'

'But we do that all the time,' she answered back. 'How often do teachers claim that a punishment is imposed to deter others from the same crime? Isn't that using some pupils as a means to an end?'

'I think what's wrong,' said Mr Jagger, drawing on his cigar, 'is not that there aren't enough university places: it's that the selection system is flawed. There are enough places, but the wrong people are filling them. The selection process isn't, and probably can't be, designed to ensure that only keen students who will persevere are chosen at the stage of "A"-Levels or scholarship exam.'

'So we're never going to be able to devise a proper selection system, is that what you're saying, Lionel?' This was Fr Bedford.

'Well, yes, it is. How can an exam or an interview predict a candidate's behaviour and attitude in two or three years' time? The number of university drop-outs is proof that the present system doesn't work, and I see no way round that.'

'I heard a radical solution the other day,' Fr Bedford said. 'It was that Oxford and Cambridge should not accept undergraduates at all. This would at a stroke leave enough room for the country's top graduates, with a track-record of academic commitment behind them.'

'But why should we put such a huge emphasis on Oxbridge?' asked Russell Smith. 'There are plenty of newer universities offering a more modern and, in many cases, a better equipped tertiary education. I think this exaggerated respect for Oxbridge is misplaced.'

'Yes, I tend to agree,' commented Frank Hendon, 'but one thing Oxford and Cambridge have got right, in my opinion, is the stress on religion and morality as mainstays of civilised behaviour. The red-bricks don't always see that.'

'On the other hand, Frank,' Mr Jagger said, 'the Oxbridge requirement of Latin for university entrance is simply old-fashioned. It's a harking back to a time that's gone for ever.'

'Can you think of a better course of study than Latin and Greek to develop the mind, train judgement and inculcate understanding for the basis of our European culture?'

'I'm perfectly certain that other disciplines are just as good at that, Frank – including my own; but my point is really that simply throwing Latin into the mix isn't going to guarantee that those most able to profit from a university education get the chance to do so.'

'What really gets me,' said Helen Mansfield, 'is that, despite all our prodding, our science candidates are just inadequate in a wider context. Let me give you an example I came across recently. A member of a prestigious firm, who was charged with working up a short-list of twenty candidates with at least one science degree each, turned the lot down. Why? Because they were badly dressed, ill-mannered, knew little outside their own discipline and, what's worse, didn't care. They gave the impression that, having passed a degree examination; it was now up to industry to offer its rewards. They regarded matters outside the degree course as their private business and were surprised, and even resentful, that more than a degree should be considered important. But you see, what the firm wanted was not just scientists, but scientists with a well-developed critical faculty, the ability to direct further work, the willingness to accept responsibility, the skill to inspire others, and so on. What would this candidate be like in five or six years' time? The selection team asked the candidates for books they had read; few could offer any apart from their textbooks. Name people who might be included amongst the twenty greatest figures of all time. They stumbled. What newspaper do you read? This or that tabloid. Ye gods!'

'Hold on a minute, Helen,' said Jagger. 'You're effectively blaming the English department for failing to encourage wider reading!'

'No, I'm not, Lionel, and you know it! It's the system that's wrong. We're encouraging our scientists to specialise too early, at the expense of their wider education. We need to implant a sense of social commitment, intellectual curiosity, wonderment, a capacity for perfection, an interest in society, and above all – and it's appropriate to use the word in the context of Mincliffe above all schools – the ability to be *charitable*.'[1]

'And do Latin and Greek do all this?' queried Jagger dryly.

'Yes, since Latin and Greek put you in touch with two of the greatest civilisations on earth.'

'Oh, yes? What's that clerihew?

A man in the position
Of the emperor Domitian
Ought to have thought twice
About being a Monster of Vice.

The Greeks and Romans were anti-feminist, bloodthirsty and rapacious, and they built societies which were inequitable, precarious and aggressive.'

'Yes, but isn't the point about the Greeks and Romans that they sowed the seeds, or laid the foundations, for essential civic virtues like efficient administration, democracy, *pietas*, nobility of purpose?' This was Frank Hendon again.

'Well,' said Mike Bedford, 'we seem to have wandered some way from the subject we started with. I've been re-reading Newman on *The Idea of a University*, in the hope of clarifying my own mind. I know it's over a century old, but I hoped for some insight into what makes a good university entrant. Do you know, Newman has nothing to say on the subject at all? I couldn't find a single instance of the word "candidate" or the word "applicant" in the entire work, and even the occurrences of the word "student" were general and vague. He seems to have no ideas on who might profit from a university education and who not.'

'That's not very fair, Mike,' said Hendon. 'You can't say everything possible about universities in one volume. But I tell you what: he has some jolly interesting things to say about Latin and its ability to discipline and shape the mind!'

'Yes, but the trouble is, we're constantly thinking of what things the university candidate needs, and the result is a list as long as your arm and getting longer: not just the classics, history and geography, comparative religion, the sciences, mathematics, English, of course, at least one foreign language, but politics, money-management, interpersonal skills, a ghastly

[1] The school's motto is *Legis plenitudo caritas*: Charity is the fulfilment of the law.

thing I heard referred to recently as citizenship, and of course practical skills like woodwork, metalwork and pottery – and so on. On top of all this he needs to demonstrate a range of useful and, if possible, intellectual hobbies, as well as umpteen personal qualities. The complete university candidate is a chimaera, and I don't mind saying so! We don't seem able to decide on what is essential and what is merely desirable.'

'And, to return to something Frank mentioned earlier, where would you say morality comes in?' said Jagger. 'Is it essential or merely desirable?'

'Morality? Essential, wouldn't you say? I mean, who wants in any community people who are dishonest, deceitful, spiteful, aggressive and so on? No, we all want as colleagues people who are open, kind, thoughtful, disciplined and helpful.'

'And how do you test morality as an essential requirement of university entrance?' There was the hint of derision in Jagger's voice.

'Well, you're right, most of a university entrance examination tests the candidate's academic skills, but the school has to write a report on the pupil, and that should include his suitability for further education. In the same way, a headmaster interviewing potential members of staff will have to judge the applicants' probity and general fitness to be educators.'

This genteel, informed and earnest conversation was brought to an abrupt end by the clamour of the school-bell - designed and constructed, incidentally, by one of the science staff in the pursuit of efficiency and good order. Jagger and Helen Mansfield found themselves walking down the corridor together. Jagger said guilelessly,

'Doing anything tonight, Helen?'

'Why?'

'I wondered whether you fancied the cinema. *The Tamarind Seed* by Blake Edwards is showing at the Regal in Evesham.'

'No. No, I don't think so, Lionel. Not tonight. Perhaps another night.'

'Look, are you seeing someone at the moment? I didn't think you were.'

'No, I'm not seeing anyone, but that doesn't mean I have to go out with you tonight.' Jagger was disappointed but kept his disappointment to himself.

That Saturday, Mincliffe hosted a sixth-form dance with senior girls from Grant College down the road. The pupils, male and female, generally regarded this educational(?) exercise with favour; by the staff, it was at most tolerated. The trouble with teenagers was that they lacked judgement. The girls dressed provocatively – or would have done if the gimlet-eyed teachers at Grant had not often intervened – while the boys lacked restraint. There were various stratagems for defeating the staff's best efforts. Girls were known to arrive decorously dressed, only to shed a garment or two later in the evening when no one was watching. Boys were known to tempt a girl outside the parts of the college set aside for the entertainment, the purpose being what they vulgarly called (please pardon the word) a 'snog' or, of course, extra physical activity feared but not seriously envisaged by the school authorities. Alcohol was forbidden, but this regulation was inevitably, and foolishly, circumvented by the less sensible or more audacious pupils. Although no one expected relationships set up on such an occasion to amount to very much, much less to be the germs of life-long romance, they were considered useful stages in the development of social skills and the management of emotion.

The ball was going well. The Grant and the Mincliffe contingents were, on the whole, civilised young people. The disc-jockey knew his business. The refreshments were more than adequate. The staff were helpful but not oppressive. The cliques of girls on the one hand and boys on the other gradually broke down as, one by one, the boys claimed a partner for themselves. The dances ensured that couples split, were lost in the general skirmish and then reformed in the accepted sequence of moves. People sat out and chatted, or walked round the dance-floor to start other conversations, or slipped into the night for a quick cigarette. Helen watched one girl in particular, a tall, willowy thing in a skimpy dress and absurdly high shoes, over-made-up and rather brassy. She seemed to be swaying, and not just because of her heels. When this creature made for the exit, Helen followed her, concerned that not all was well. The changing-rooms attached to the gym, which doubled as the dance-floor, had been made over to the visitors. Helen followed the girl in but was not in time to prevent her collapsing on the floor. Walking quickly back into the gym, Helen caught hold of the first man she saw, who happened to be Lionel Jagger, pulled him urgently by the arm rather than shout in his ear above the din of the records and led him into the changing-rooms. Together they gathered the girl up and carried her to the infirmary, which was in the main building, up a flight of stairs and part-way along a corridor. The girl had vomited and was deathly white; her eyes were closed. A bell summoned matron from the depths and, suspecting a misuse of drugs, matron summoned an ambulance and asked Helen to inform the Grant staff of this turn of events. Having handed matters over to their visiting colleagues, Helen and Lionel stood facing each other in the corridor outside the gym. The noise of the dance in oblivious progress percolated loudly through from within. Helen, thinking of the sick girl botching up her life, and touched by her vulnerable and fallen innocence, was yet sufficiently aware to see the amorous intent in Lionel's eyes, and something inside her half responded. After all, he was not bad to look at: quite pleasant, in fact. He had broad shoulders, a muscular figure, large, shapely hands. His candid face and well-proportioned features were surmounted by a crop of boyish, curly hair. She did not wish to be alone in life. She could do worse, she thought, than cosy up to him, figuratively speaking, for want of the love of her youth, her lost Jed. Lionel, sensing a warming in his regard, laid a careful hand on her arm and suggested a nightcap after the dance. He had a bottle of something suitable, and he would happily escort her home afterwards. She accepted.

Lionel Jagger occupied one of several cottages in Mincliffe grounds, not far from the main drive. It was not large - comfortable for a bachelor or a couple, but perhaps a bit of a squeeze beyond that - but it was snug and handy. Lionel ushered Helen into the living-room, took her coat and brought back a bottle of Drambuie that an acquaintance had given him, together with two suitable glasses. He turned a bar of the fire on, more for cheer's sake than because the night was cool, and a tentative conversation began. This was the first time the two had been so placed, man to woman, face to face *remotis arbitris*, as our Roman friends have it. They sat in silence for a moment, pondering the opening move. Both were aware that something was beginning.

'Tell me about yourself, Helen, where you come from, your family, that sort of thing.'

'Not much to tell, really,' she replied. 'I haven't had what you'd call a dramatic or exciting life. I'm a Worcester girl, born and bred, one of three girls. My father, who's dead now, worked as an overhead lines engineer for a Worcester company, and Mum's a lettings officer with the council. I was lucky enough to get to grammar school and go on to uni.'

'Where?'

'Nottingham.'

'Did you like it?'

'Yeah, not bad.'

'Then on to the job market, I suppose?'

'Yeah, but again I was lucky. I got a job almost straight away at Droitwich High School – a good school, but somehow I always knew I wanted to move on at some stage, before getting too dug in. Then this job at Mincliffe came up, and, knowing I was ready for a move, I applied, and – well, here I am!'

'Do you like it?'

'Yes, very much.'

'So you're here to stay. You live just down the road, don't you?'

'Yes, I rent a semi in Murcot Road. Not special but convenient.'

'Aren't you lonely?'

'Maybe, but then you're on your own, too: what about you? Are you lonely?'

'Lonely?' He appeared to turn the word over in his mind, savouring its resonances and connotations. 'I'm on my own, certainly. I have what you might call bachelor accommodation, but we do spend all our working lives surrounded by people, you know. The classroom is hardly a lonely place!'

'Yes, I know that,' she said, 'of course I do, but deep down, don't you feel the need for – well, for someone special?'

'Yes, I suppose I do. From the way you're talking, you obviously do too.'

''Uman nature, innit? Not many of us are single by desire.' She gave a pallid smile. 'I had a boyfriend once. I can't seem to get beyond him.'

'What happened?'

'Not sure. We grew up next door to each other. Jed, his name was; smashing bloke: tall, lithe, handsome – to me, at any rate. We'd always got on - you know, as youngsters. The relationship seemed natural; it had always been there, ever since I could remember. I regarded him as a brother more than anything else. Then as I got older, I began to wonder whether there might not be more to it. I fell in love with him, I suppose, that's the long and the short of it.' She paused to gaze wistfully into the distance. 'I dreamt of having him to myself for ever. An immature, girlish dream, I daresay, but it gave me vitality and warmth and hope. Then it all petered out. I came home after the first term up at Nottingham, and he'd changed. I can't properly describe the way he'd changed. He was just as solicitous and kind and gentle as before, but he'd grown – how shall I put it? – distant, absent-minded, almost floating in detachment from ordinary, everyday concerns. He'd become *self-sufficient*, I think that may be the best word, as if he had no need of anybody else. He'd matured in a particular direction, and I didn't like it. There'd never been any commitment between us: the love had probably all been on my side, and I'd never told him how I felt. I just presumed he'd always be there, living next door to us. Then one day he said he was taking up a post as warden of some nature reserve off the west coast of Scotland and that he didn't expect to be getting home very often. He didn't ask me to go with him – why should he? – and he just vanished; disappeared one day, taking a suitcase. That was it: I've never seen him again; and yet I hunger for him more than ever. Why can't I get him out of my head?'

'How long ago was this?'

'Seven years – seven interminable years,' and the words contained a whole lifetime of longing. 'Look, Lionel, thanks for the drink. I must be going. Don't worry about seeing me home: it's only a few hundred yards. See you Monday.' And she was gone. Jagger felt suddenly lonely.

Two

A week later, Lionel took Helen out for a meal in Evesham. He chose the Evesham Hotel, which, he told her, ran a very creditable restaurant. It was a cold evening. Helen was well beyond the teenage fashion of appearing on such occasions, on the grounds that a cardigan or coat was demeaning, wearing the minimum. The restaurant was quite busy, which pleased them, since to undertake serious wooing in a place devoid of character and mood was likely to lead nowhere. I say 'serious wooing', but it is doubtful whether Helen saw it for what it was. She lay in a cocoon of aching loss which prevented her from being open to new possibilities. It might have made the independent observer impatient. Jagger was attentive and gentlemanly. He saw to it that her coat was hung up by the door, that she was given first choice of a seat in the lounge, offered a drink and made to feel cosseted. They talked of this and that, mainly recent school events, in an unforced and undemanding way, sipping their drinks in quiet anticipation of a friendly meal together. This was Helen's first even vaguely amorous date since her university days, and the novelty of it was not lost on her as the warmth and friendliness of the room took hold. Lionel's attentions were working on her to the extent of making the occasion more than just minor. For his part, he was unsure of where he wished the relationship to go: was it a pleasant evening out between colleagues, or a serious effort to win a lady's interest? Thinking cynically that he would not be the loser if he put effort into laying solid foundations for a significant association, he adopted the frame of mind of one who would a-wooing go. He was also unscrupulous enough to see the evening as a stepping-stone to physical satisfaction; this unworthy thought lurked in the unchivalrous antechambers of his psyche.

They were called to their table and took their places, Jagger settling her chair for her: no gesture of gallantry was omitted. They both had salmon and tarragon fish-cakes to start with, she following this with grilled rib-eye steak, he with roast breast of chicken. For dessert, she opted for crême brûlé, while he had hot bananas in a rum sauce. Cheese followed, *more britannico.*

Jagger had, on the wine-waiter's recommendation, chosen a Barolo, which proved a very acceptable accompaniment for the two of them. Helen began to feel, almost despite herself, that she wanted to get to know her companion better.

'Lionel,' she said, 'I've told you my life-story, such as it is. What's yours?'

'Nothing to it, really,' he replied, swallowing a mouthful of chicken. 'I'm a Norfolk man – and no, nothing to do with "normal for Norfolk". I went to school in Norwich and then on to university for a combined English and drama degree.'

'Where?'

'University of Windsor – that's in Detroit, by the way, not on the River Thames – did a five-year masters degree and loved it. I didn't fancy working in the US, though, so I came home and got a job with the newly opened Belgrade Theatre in Coventry. After a few years of rep work, I changed tack, and here I am – a hack worker at the chalk-face, single, unattached and eminently eligible!'

'Says you!' Helen commented, smiling. She scrutinised his boyish face and saw only honesty and manliness.

'How old are you?'

'Twenty-eight,' he said. 'And you?'

'Twenty-seven.'

'Made for each other,' he said.

'Jumping the gun a bit, aren't you? I hardly know you, and while it's nice to be in your company for an evening, I'm not sure we should make a habit of it.'

After the meal, they elected to sit back in the lounge with their coffees. Jagger offered a liqueur, and they both had a Grand Marnier. Jagger knew that the evening would cost him a week's salary, but the words of Shakespeare sprang, as ever, to his mind:

> We must take the current when it serves,
>
> Or lose our ventures.

In the light of her last comment at the table, however, he revised his expectation of any activity later on beyond a chaste goodnight: better to bide his time. The conversation came round to Destiny: was there such a thing? Were humans the playthings of Fate or actors responsible for their own character in a loosely improvised drama?

'Do you know Goethe's *The Elective Affinities*?' Jagger asked Helen. 'It's a good example of fatalism in literature, and because the title was pinched from a textbook on chemistry, it would probably appeal to you too.'

'No, I don't know it: what's it about?'

'Well, here's the story in a nutshell. The story centres on four characters: a couple, Baron Edward - his surname is never revealed - and his wife Charlotte, on the one hand, the baron's friend the Captain and his wife's niece Ottilie on the other. When the Baron hears that his friend the Captain has fallen on hard times, he invites him to the castle to stay until he can find another job. Bad move. At the same time, the baroness invites her niece to stay. Another bad move. Inevitably – but that's the point of the story - the Captain falls in love with Charlotte and Edward with Ottilie. Edward flees to give himself time to think; the Captain goes away. During their absence, Ottilie is responsible for the death by accidental drowning of Charlotte's infant son Otto (born, we are led to believe, of Charlotte's adultery with the Captain). Ottilie goes into a decline and dies. When he hears the news, Edward dies of a broken heart. He and Ottilie are buried together in the castle vault. End of novel. A tear-jerker. Almost as bad as *Werther*. Did Goethe intend to justify the break-up of the baron's marriage, on the grounds that the baron had no choice in the matter: it was "destined"? Or does Edward's death signify divine punishment for breaking his marriage vows?'

'Well, what do you think?'

'I don't know what Goethe had in mind. The book includes this passage, if I can remember it properly:

> There are certain things [the author has Ottilie say] which Destiny proposes stubbornly.

- and I remember the exact word Goethe uses there: *hartnäckig*, "stiff-neckedly", because it has always seemed to me such a pitiless word-

> Reason and virtue [she goes on], duty and everything sacred are powerless: what seems right to Destiny must take place, even though it doesn't seem right to us; and in the end Destiny wins, whatever we do.

Now isn't that just too appalling? I mean, it reduces us to marionettes, pieces on a chess-board. One surely can't reduce human emotion to chemical reactions. I remember thinking the same thing about something I once read in Francis Galton – you know, the man who discovered the uniqueness of fingerprints back in the last century. In a disgraceful phrase, he refers to the *vox populi* as "the utterance of a mob of nobodies"! Sorry: I'm not boring you am I, Helen?'

'Not at all,' she said sincerely. 'Go on: I want to know how Galton justifies his statement.'

'Well, that's the point: he doesn't – well, not convincingly, to my way of thinking. His thesis is that the vast majority of people have a natural tendency to shrink from the responsibility of standing and acting alone – and remember that, like Goethe, Galton was a scientist. He proves it by likening human behaviour to that of a herd of wild South African oxen! Each herd, apparently, is numerically determined by the amount of grazing land that'll support it and the size that makes for best protection from predators. Weak members are weeded out by processes of natural selection, and to prevent the herd from getting too small owing to the attacks of big cats on straying members, forty-nine out of fifty oxen are sufficiently gregarious to keep the herd together. The fiftieth is the leader who manages the herd. Humans are similar, he argues – but on what grounds he doesn't make clear. Most people are, in his words, "willing slaves to tradition, authority and custom" and are characterised by a "rareness of free and original thought". Now isn't all that just too depressing?'

'Where does he say that?' asked Helen. 'I might like to read it.'

'I can't remember the title of the essay, but it's one of those collected in his *Inquiries into human faculty*, a sort of forerunner to *The Naked Ape*, I suppose one could call it. What gets me is the way scientists like Galton pontificate about this, that and t'other but really have no proof. Sorry: perhaps I shouldn't be talking like this to a biologist!'

'No, no, carry on! Science no more has all the answers than religion has.'

'Huh, that's a provocative sentiment from a member of staff at a Catholic school! You do believe in religion, I hope?'

'Yes, of course, but perhaps this is neither the time nor the place to be taking it further. I feel very comfortable after a good meal - thanks very much, Lionel - and I don't want to spoil it with an argument. Another time, perhaps.'

The conversation wound on; other diners and some of the residents came and went. The fire was topped up from time to time by some hotel minion, and at half-past ten Helen said she was tired and thought she'd like to leave. Jagger paid, trying not to register his alarm at the size of the bill, and then drove his guest back to Murcot.

'Fancy a night-cap at my place?' he said.

'I don't think so,' she said. 'Nice of you to offer, but I'm just too tired. Thanks for a lovely evening, Lionel. See you Monday.' She reached over and kissed him lightly on the cheek.

The term proceeded. A teacher's work-day does not end when the final bell sounds at four o'clock. He or she has then to clear up, keep on top of the marking, check preparation for the morrow's classes, or perhaps attend a meeting or a school activity, or see a pupil for an encouraging talk and some quick private tuition, or take time to listen to an anxious parent. Conducting a romance is no easy undertaking in these circumstances, but Jagger saw to it that he spent as much time with Helen as possible, in breaks and at weekends. If other members of staff noticed, nothing was said: all too busy on their own account, no doubt. Helen did not register any aversion to his continued attentions. Eventually, as these things must, the holidays came round. Helen spent a few days at home before going to her parents' in Worcester for Christmas, while Jagger went off to Switzerland for some skiing with friends. For New Year he went to Norfolk to stay with a cousin. It transpired, therefore, that Helen and he did not meet over the holidays except in its last days. Although both wished to spend time preparing their work for the new term – Helen partly because she was still relatively new to the job, Jagger because his headship of department gave him extra responsibility – they managed time together. They walked in the countryside, went to the cinema in Evesham and had a coffee in Broadway. The relationship was relaxed and comfortable and seemed to be developing 'normally', if such a word has meaning in this context.

The spring term is generally regarded with some dread by the teaching profession. Any novelty that accompanied the opening term of the year has long since worn away, and the weather is likely to be cheerless. It is a question of a constant daily grind to prepare pupils for examinations in the following term. Pupils are at their least receptive (on the other hand, this could be regarded as a normal state of affairs). The only break in their relationship was at half-term, when Helen went off to the north of England to spend a few days with an ailing aunt. Jagger's birthday fell towards the end of term, and Helen insisted on taking him out for a meal. Jagger protested that no gentleman could allow that, but she countered with two arguments – three, really. Firstly, he paid for most of their outings, and it was only just that she should bear her part of the expense when occasion demanded it. Secondly, it was his birthday, not hers. Thirdly, it would give her pleasure to treat him. Yielding gracefully, Jagger allowed himself on the evening of his birthday to be taken to dinner at the Crown and Trumpet in Broadway, a seventeenth-century inn that Helen thought would bring suitable gravitas to the occasion. (The street-sign shows a trumpeter with his mouth poised at his instrument, from which is pendant a banner depicting a crown. How a royal trumpeter came to be associated with this inn is irrelevant to the quality of the meal that Helen and Jagger enjoyed that night.)

The two had now known each other for six months in, shall we say, more than a strictly professional capacity. Helen had warmed to Lionel, to the extent of considering his presence at her side not just a transient part of her life. He was good-looking, companionable, well-read, intelligent and an effective and popular teacher. Neither was getting younger, and she could do worse than hitch her wagon to his star. (Whence does Wickfield dredge up these dreadful metaphors? I think he had mistaken its meaning anyway.) For his part, Jagger was increasingly intent on claiming Helen as his own. He loved the way she looked, the way she walked, the way she spoke. Here, he told himself, was one of the world's natural graces, fashioned, not by the hand of man in an attempt to capture the charm and loveliness of the ultimate Woman, but by nature herself as a declaration of what womanhood could be like. He allowed himself to be increasingly besotted with her, so that his waking moments were filled with visions of her, dressed and undressed, until he came to regard marriage as the natural result of their relationship. When the appropriate moment came, he would propose.

That evening was a memorably pleasant occasion. The restaurant was full. Most of the diners were couples, but there were several families, a group of six women enjoying a night out, and two men in suits deep in conversation. Helen and Jagger were placed towards the edge of the room. She wore a black plaited halter dress, with gathers at the front, that showed her legs to good advantage, while he had on an Oxford blue evening suit with a white dress shirt and black bow tie. They made a handsome couple. They ordered, he allowing her to dictate his meal, on the grounds that she was beginning to know his tastes more surely than he himself, and that anyway, because it was her treat, she wanted it to be perfect. The wine was French. Occasionally his hand wandered on to hers and lay there; or their eyes locked, Helen's a vivid blue offset with cunning make-up, his dark brown with the depth and brilliance of a cat's-eye chrysoberyl. They chatted of this and that, spontaneously, effortlessly, an intelligent conversation of two people rejoicing in the vigour and versatility of each other's minds. Helen was a biologist, but she had wide interests outside her own discipline. Jagger had read widely in all sorts of areas: novels, of course, poetry and plays – he had grown up with them, they were the materials of his job, his head teemed with remembered quotations – but also art, history, language, politics, philosophy, sport, music: there was little in which he could show no interest at all.

The conversation turned to the relationship between an institution and the freedom of the individuals who belong to it. Jagger appealed to Herodotus.

'His view was that history proved that Athenian democracy worked in a way that Athenian despotism didn't. Under the despots, the Athenians were no better militarily than their neighbours. As soon as they threw off the oppressors, they became the finest fighters in the world.'

'And how does he explain that?'

'Well, he says that under a despotism, the citizens malingered out of a feeling that they were working for a master, whereas, when they had gained their freedom, they all felt, individually, that they were working to their own advantage.'

'And you go along with that, I suppose?'

'Yes, I do. You see, the motto of institutions - of societies which take on a life independent of that of the individuals that compose it – is "Carry on regardless". They ask themselves not Why? but only How? Their concern is to survive, to endure, not to promote the welfare of the members, by change if necessary. All long-established institutions have a vested interest in stability and a corresponding fear of change as a threat to their identity. If the institution isn't the same as what it was, what on earth is it? So institutions, of their very nature, oppress. The individual who steps out of line, or who voices criticism, or who expresses dissatisfaction, has to be disciplined, to prevent diffusion of the rot. And of course, when I say "institution", I mean the men and women, if there is more than one, who together constitute the authorities, those in charge, those who give orders and ensure obedience to them. What they don't see is that they are simply repeating, inevitably, the mistakes of all their predecessors. They will carry on bolstering up their own positions, as guardians of what they perceive to be truth and justice and stability, until their petty, blinkered little selves are swept away in revolution or invasion.'

'You're getting quite worked up, Lionel!'

'Yes, I probably am, with good cause! There's worse, you know. Read Bertrand Russell. "It's no use to attempt any bolstering up of institutions based on authority," he says, "since all such institutions involve injustice" – a great work, that, his *Principles of Social Reconstruction*! So you see, where Herodotus argued that non-democratic authority didn't work properly, Russell argued that it's positively harmful, and his arguments are, to my mind, persuasive.'

'So what's the answer?'

'Part of the answer is certainly education. Do you know Ivan Illich, the maverick Catholic priest? He's an amazing thinker – but I won't go into that here. You probably know him anyway. Now he says somewhere, I think in *The Celebration of Awareness*, that institutions create certainties. That's how they survive. "Taken seriously," he comments, and these are the words I remember particularly, "certainties deaden the heart and shackle the imagination." Certainties deaden the heart: and that from a priest of the Catholic Church the mere statement of whose dogmas – irreversible teachings - would fill a substantial volume! One purpose of education, therefore, says Illich, is to unravel certainties, to liberate the imagination so that people can envisage other and better ways of managing their affairs or of understanding their place in the cosmos.'

'But the purpose of education as we practise it is to give the children reliable information,' Helen protested. 'I teach them the principles of biology. It's not my job to teach them to doubt and question. You teach them the rules of English grammar or the proper structure of an essay. You can't go round urging them to question and rebel!'

'Well, not little ones, possibly, but the teacher has always to keep in mind that the purpose of his work is *eventually* to get the pupils to think for themselves; all he teaches is provisional, because he hopes the pupil will revise and amend and adjust, perhaps even sweep away, what he's learning *now* in order to put something better in its place *then*.'

'But places of learning can be just as trammelling as political institutions! Simply setting up an educational system and running it doesn't guarantee any of the qualities you're talking about.'

'You're right of course, and the answer to that is vigilance, constant vigilance. Any educational establishment has always to refine its aims so that pupils' learning comes first – and I mean learning in the sense of *re*consideration and improvement.'

'You'll make yourself unpopular at school if you come out with all this in public, Lionel.'

'Huh, I don't think I'm very popular with the school at the moment. The president thinks I'm out to rock the boat.'

'And are you?'

'Yes, I suppose I am. Mincliffe is good as schools go, but we're not yet a national leader in educational thinking. That's what I think we should be: a leader!'

At the close of the evening, Lionel, whose car they had used, dropped Helen off at her house on the way to his. They kissed: a warm, even passionate, embrace, that spoke of their growing intimacy, of a meeting of bodies and not just of minds.

Three

Jagger, thinking that a proposal of marriage would now meet with a favourable response, began to decide on the best occasion. Of course, he reasoned, any time would do: the middle of a school term is no obstacle to settling on one's companion for life. Contrariwise, a proposal during the holidays would speak into a void, without one's professional colleagues to offer congratulations and solidarity. On the other hand, it would not do to propose when Helen was tired or vexed, enduring the hassle of a term in full swing. On the other hand again, the families could be better involved during the holidays. Jagger was sorely exercised. He plumped eventually for a Saturday afternoon. He planned to suggest a country walk round Alderton Hill with a cream tea at Beckford or possibly Tewksbury. He would then propose. Before I tell you about that, however, you need some account of the staff-meeting which caused such disturbance as Mincliffe's hallowed walls had rarely experienced.

On Wednesday, it was. The president had the good sense generally to limit the monthly staff-meeting to one hour: what could not be decided in the space of an hour, he declared, would have to wait or be decided in another forum. However keen and fit, no one can support a long meeting at the end of a working day without loss of alertness and efficiency. Like Topsy, Mincliffe had just growed over the years. One of the casualties of the process of expansion was the original chapel, which, as chapel, had outgrown its place in the establishment and had been converted many years before into the staff-room. It was a spacious and lofty room, but narrow, in accordance with the liturgical ideas of the time, with an unmistakeable ecclesiastical air despite years of use as a meeting- and work-place. The chairs were arranged in rows down the length of the room, the president and vice-president occupying the centre of the long side, under the gothic windows. The item on the agenda which caused the tension was the final one, a proposal to alter the terms of the lay-staff contract, so that the retiring age would be fixed at sixty rather than sixty-five. The idea was to give the school the option of bidding farewell to a teacher at sixty, if it so desired, or alternatively of inviting him or her to continue for a year, and then for a further year, and so on. It was, of course, designed to work to the school's advantage. Whatever the item on the agenda had been, however, Jagger would have used it to publicise his ideas on how an institution should operate: the planned change to the contract was merely a peg on which to hang his vision of the school's future.

'Fr President,' he declaimed at an appropriate moment, 'may I register my disagreement? It's not that I object to the proposal in itself: I object to the way in which it's being imposed unilaterally.'

'I see, Mr Jagger,' the president said. 'Can you explain more precisely what you mean?' The president, Fr Alan Jackson was a tall, slim man, with a shock of white hair crowning a benevolent face, nearer sixty than fifty, with an easy air of command.

'Yes, certainly,' said Jagger, now confident that he had the eager ear of the entire assembly. He could probably count on the support of his fellow lay-teachers and on the opposition of the religious staff, but at that moment his intention was merely to make a point: to sow the seeds of a small insurgence.

'In any establishment with pretensions to Christian fraternity, the members who make it up must be not passive recipients of social life but its creators.'

'Isn't that a bit bald as it stands, Mr Jagger? Have you any justification for it?' the president asked mildly.

'Yes, lots, Fr President, but allow me to instance just two arguments, if you will. One is this. St Augustine says that God speaks to every member of the Church, from the bishops right down to the last of the faithful. All right, I admit that the context is a particular one: in his argument against the Pelagians, he's defending the Old Testament *Book of Wisdom* as authoritative. God himself, he asserts, has allowed the book to be heard by all members of the Christian community - and I can give you the Latin - *ab episcopis usque ad extremos laicos fideles*; but my point stands, I believe: God doesn't talk to the laity just through the bishops, at second remove. I also like a sentiment to which Augustine resorts in one of his sermons. The Church is like a mother, he says: she loves to nourish her children but does not wish them to remain children. My second argument is that, in his Radio Message for 1944, Pope Pius XII, of blessed memory, acknowledged that democracy is a fruit of the gospel. I'm sorry I haven't got the original words in my head!' Some titters followed this admission. 'If democracy is a fruit of the gospel, we should be a democracy!'

'Is that it, Mr Jagger?'

'Only in part, Fr President. I don't want to take up too much time at this meeting, but if you will allow me to comment briefly on the idea of obedience, which will perhaps explain better what I'm getting at, I should be grateful. Obedience is usually conceived as doing what one is told, and there are usually two arguments deployed in its favour. Firstly, any society must be structured and organised; if everyone did as he pleased, there would be confusion. Secondly, authority, all things being equal, is God-given: lawful superiors, whether parents, employers or civic or political authorities, are sanctioned by God to coordinate the society. In the notorious and surprising phrase of that arch-provocateur, Adolf Harnack, "it is only when he obeys that the Catholic approaches God". Now I want to question that entire mentality.'

'Is this going to take long, Mr Jagger?' the president asked, perhaps a little wearily.

'Well, I hope not, Fr President, but if I'm to say anything worthwhile, I must be allowed a little space.'

'Very well. Proceed.'

'As I was saying, obedience is commonly misconceived as a passive attitude of doing what one is told. My view is that no instruction or law can command obedience unless the subject has contributed to it. May I quote St Cyprian? "No decree can be firm," he says, "which shall not appear to have the consent of numbers." That, from a bishop, is pretty good, I should say. It seems to me that there is no compelling reason why unity and order should call for submission to a head. Cooperation between members whose destiny and welfare are inextricably entangled would seem to satisfy the requirements equally. The symbol of unity in the service of an overriding aim is therefore not necessarily the pyramid: it could be the round table.' Jagger could sense rather than hear murmurs of approval from some of his colleagues - and murmurs of dissent elsewhere in his audience. Everybody was certainly listening, even if the speaker was polarising them. He resumed his argument.

'Now this may be an extreme formulation, but this is the conclusion to which these and other arguments tend: the only structure that can be tolerated in a school with any pretensions to a Christian ethos is one which arises from within the whole community. Such a structure exists as a reasoned manifestation of the members' concern to order their affairs to the more effective education of the young. We should really be working - and I mean not just casually but urgently - towards a state of affairs in which schools establish the equality of all their members.'

'And does that include the pupils, Mr Jagger?' the president asked. 'Are the pupils to be part of this "democracy", as you call it, as well?'

'Certainly, Fr President, to the extent to which their age qualifies them. May I appeal to the *Letter to the Ephesians*? In chapter four, Paul, or the unknown author if it isn't Paul, urges the community to be united. Now it's significant, to me at any rate, that he doesn't appeal to a centralised figure of authority, round whom everyone else should rally. He doesn't say anything about a central figure of authority representing Christ. Instead he points to the difference of gift, and therefore of function, within the total community, and to the need for mature cooperation in working towards what he calls the unity of faith.' There was a ripple of displeasure from members of the religious staff, and Jagger realised that he was not going to win the argument there and then, or even be able to expound it satisfactorily. He must be content to lay the foundations of further discussion.

'Perhaps I should stop there, Fr President,' he therefore added. 'But may I just finish with an apt *pensée* from Pascal? There are some, he says, who submit blindly, unable to see when personal judgement is required.'

'Yes, Mr Jagger,' the president commented dryly, 'but in that same paragraph he also excoriates those who doubt everything, unable to see when *submission* is required. And with that, ladies and gentlemen, colleagues all, I suggest we draw this meeting to a close. I should like to thank Mr Jagger for his intervention: undoubtedly he is always interesting to listen to, and he has given us food for thought. One day, maybe, say an in-service training day, we can ask him to expand on his ideas. Perhaps I can have a word with you after this meeting, Mr Jagger, at your convenience?'

Before the end of the meeting, one or two other members of staff had also muttered words of discontent, notably the new PE teacher, Ralph Maginniss, and Robin Davidson, teacher of German and French.

The little group of Institute staff gathered in Br Andy Gallagher's room were incensed. Br Gallagher taught chemistry. Also present were Fr Bill Hinchcliffe, head of music, Fr Stephen Duffin, head of history, Fr Hendon, the bursar, and Br Piers Ellison, a retired teacher of English. They sat around rubbing their hands and shaking their heads.

'It won't do, you know,' said Fr Hinchcliffe. 'This sort of talk isn't seemly.'

'What got me,' said Br Gallagher, 'is the nerve of the fellow. He talked as if we had no theology. We're meant to be the experts. He's a teacher of English, for heaven's sake: what does he know about theology? He spouted Augustine and Pius XII and *Ephesians* at us as if we were children in one of his classes.'

'Steady on, Andy,' Fr Hendon said. 'We should be glad Jagger's got a bit of theology. There's no ban on the laity reading Augustine, you know.'

'No, there isn't,' Br Ellison put in. 'But it was the way he talked. "I want to question that entire mentality,"' he mimicked. 'Does he, indeed?'

'Is a routine staff-meeting the proper forum for big discussions like that?' questioned Fr Hinchcliffe. 'I agree with you, Bill, Jagger was just too cocky for words. He was showing off in front of the assembled staff: Augustine this, Harnack that, Paul the other. Who does he think he is?'

'Well, I can't see where else he could bring up such topics. The only thing I should say is that he should perhaps have informed Fr President first. If he set out to cause trouble, it was an immature intervention, but I don't object to bringing up wider topics at a staff-meeting. All too often staff-meetings get bogged down in details, and we risk losing sight of the bigger picture.'

'Well, in my view,' declared Br Ellison, 'he ought to go. If the fellow's got any decency, he'll hand in his resignation and push off; leave us in peace. How the school is run is not his business. He's here to teach, dammit, and all he's doing is upsetting folk. Let him stick to Shakespeare and the rest of the "O"-Level syllabus!'

'What if one of us had come out with such arguments?' persisted Frank Hendon. 'Are you annoyed because he's only a layman?'

'Layman or priest, no one has the right to criticise the organisation of the school at a public meeting, without a by-your-leave or prior notification.'

Jagger was not dismayed by the summons to present himself at the headmaster's office. A teacher could not be sacked merely for speaking at a staff meeting. Even if he, Jagger, *were* sacked, martyrdom would be acceptable in the cause of truth. The head's office was on the ground floor, at the front of the building. Two doors gave on to the corridor, four windows on to the driveway. It was well, if not handsomely, furnished, with décor and furniture designed both to soothe the well-disposed and intimidate the recalcitrant.

'Ah, yes, do take a seat, Jagger,' the president said affably. 'Now then, what's all this about?'

'It's not "about" anything, Fr President. I merely wanted to make a point.'

'About the way this school is run?'

'Well, yes, in a way, but my remarks apply to all Christian establishments, not just this school.'

'Do they, now? You wouldn't want to be starting a mutiny, by any chance? What would that achieve?'

'No, not a mutiny, but a revolution in the way we think about Christian communities.'

'The weight of tradition is against you, I fear, and also, I venture to say, the weight of present-day opinion in scholastic and ecclesiastical circles.'

'You will know St Cyprian's indignant cry, father: "Is custom to be of more value than truth? *quasi consuetudo major sit veritate*".'

'My, we are well-read, Mr Jagger! Cyprian, again! The fact is, your remarks were felt by my colleagues in the Institute to be unsettling. You're rocking the boat. It's not your words we object to, but the subversive attitude behind them. Reasoned argument is one thing, rebellion another.' He paused. 'I hope you're not unsettling the pupils in your classes.' He paused again. 'Unfortunately, as an English teacher, you have occasion to engage the class in a wide variety of discussions. Have you ever talked to them about, er, obedience and democracy? about the subject of your remarks this afternoon?'

'Well, I don't recall exactly. Quite often topics arise spontaneously out of the pupils' work. I like to think there's a lot of spontaneity in my classes, father, and in any case, surely the object of education is to get the kids to think for themselves.'

'It is, of course it is, but perhaps most of that is best left to the universities, when students have a better grasp of the wider picture.'

'Yes, but you've got to get them started. We want to produce inquiring minds. Surely you agree with that, father?'

'Yes, but what I'm trying to get across to you, Lionel, is that there is a world of difference between reasoned questioning and the bolshie desire to abandon convention. May I quote an article from a couple of years ago by the Jesuit Fr de Lubac?' Here he reached behind him to gather a slim volume off a shelf. Jagger noted that it was an issue of *Nouvelle Revue Théologique*. The head flicked through it. 'I'm sure you're fluent in French, Lionel, as in many other things, so there's no need for me to translate. Our writer says ... let me see ... yes, here we are. He's talking about the Church, of course:

> Tous sont appelés, dans son sein, à la sainteté. Pour les guider dans cette marche, le Seigneur a donné à son Église une constitution hiérarchique, le collège épiscopal dont le pape est le chef ayant la triple mission d'enseigner, de sanctifier et de gouverner. Or, de divers côtés, on semble ne vouoloir retenir de cette doctrine que l'ideé, ou plutôt l'expression, de "peuple de Dieu", pour transformer l'Église en une vaste démocratie ... On critique ce qu'on appelle "l'Église institutionelle" au nom d'un idéal de christianisme amorphe aussi contraire à tout réalisme qu'à la foi catholique et à l'histoire des origines. Par là ne sont pas seulement encouragés des abus et des désordres pratiques: c'est la constitution divine de l'Église, c'est son essence même, telle qu'elle existait dès le premier jour, qui est atteinte.

May I invite you to ponder his main message, that the Church is not a secular, but a religious, indeed divine, society, and that therefore different considerations apply? I should perhaps add that de Lubac cites no less a theologian than Congar in his support. Well, what do you say: is this the sort of thing you would be comfortable with talking about in class? We can't have you preaching heresy or insurrection in class, I hope you agree.'

'I'm not trying to unsettle the boys, father, I'm merely trying to get them to think. Most of the time they just imbibe knowledge, mop up facts, who said this, who did that. I want them to have views of their own.'

'I can understand that; I can even admire it, but let's be clear, Lionel, that from now on you must avoid contentious subjects like democracy in the Church or in the school. There must be a million other things you can talk about in class. I owe it to the governors and parents, and indeed to the boys themselves, to protect the pupils from the sort of belligerent stuff you came out with this afternoon.'

'And if I don't?'

'That is not the sort of attitude I appreciate, Mr Jagger. The governors would support me whole-heartedly if it ever came to a show-down between us two: but I do hope it won't come to that. Please be sensible, and we shall rub along fine. I appreciate the work you do in the school, both in and out of class, but I cannot allow our ethos to be questioned, much less endangered. Do I make myself clear?'

'Very well, father. I agree.'

The debate ground on, in little groups for the most part. There seemed to be three main questions, as the staff, both religious and lay, discussed Jagger's intervention at Wednesday's staff-meeting: was it proper for a new member of staff to have introduced the topic? was a routine staff-meeting the proper forum for such a topic? was what Jagger said in any way correct? Opinion was divided on all three questions, and the lines of division coincided neither with religious status nor with age. One might wish to argue that the somewhat enclosed atmosphere of a boarding-school exaggerated the importance of the debate. The swapping of learned references - to biblical letters, fathers of the church, papal messages and philosophers - was a shade recherché to have enthused members of less pressurised establishments. At stake, said some, was the educational theory behind the Institute's schools, of which Mincliffe was only one example world-wide. That theory, elaborated in a spirit of faith and charity and honed over many years of pedagogical practice, was not to be exploded in a minute by some jumped-up *parvenu* intent on causing trouble. Others said that the debate was a side-line and would pass and that it was a mistake to accord it any but transient importance. I abstain from offering a view, since my duty as chronicler is to record the facts, not speculate on their fitness. Let me, however, just inform you of a difficulty at this point. Wickfield's notes here are a jumble of erasures, corrections, hieroglyphics and arrows. He seems to be offering opinions of his own on the three questions debated by the Mincliffe staff. Now since in my view Wickfield has on these matters, as probably on any others, no opinion worth entertaining, I am making no effort to construe his scribblings. I shall, however, for the sake of completeness, offer *my* opinions, which I advance to you as part of the package, so to speak. They are: yes, despite being a new member of staff, Jagger had every right to speak: even new-comers belong fully to the community, from the moment of their appointment; I see no reason why a routine staff-meeting should not be the vehicle of such debate; and yes, his views point in the right direction. On the other hand, it would have been judicious to discuss them with the headmaster first. How is that for a spot of homely, impromptu wisdom?

Four

The boys knew nothing of all this, of course, and they would not have cared if they had. The life of school-boys rarely (if my own modest experience, many years ago, is any guide) encompasses the finer points of pedagogical theory. Their concerns are for the mundane and the practical, the immediate and the functional. Staff talked and chalked their way through the Thursday and the Friday of that week, discoursing learnedly (one presumes) on the details of osmosis and the War of Jenkins' Ear, of mathematical identities and Charles Dickens' later novels. Helen Mansfield and Lionel Jagger met in the staff-room at the end of the school day on Friday.

'OK for tomorrow, Helen?' Jagger asked casually.

'Yes, fine,' she replied, probably all unsuspecting. 'The weather looks like being fine, so no need for winter woollies or sou'westers.'

'I'll pick you up at about one. Will that do?'

'Yep, I'll be there. Have you fixed the route?'

'Well, there's no easy way, and if we stick to footpaths we'll be wandering all over the place. Now if we head for Aston Somerville on the footpath, then switch to the road from Aston through Wormington to Dumbleton, and from there take the track through the woods to Alderton, and then on to Beckford by road, that makes eight and a half miles by my calculation – probably a bit long, there and back in an afternoon. So I suggest we cycle as far as Wormington, leave our bikes at the church, and then do the rest of the route as already suggested. That will give us about five and a half miles to walk to Beckford, and then five and a half miles back to our bikes. That's more manageable, I think. What do you say?'

'I'm game,' she said. 'I'm looking forward to some exercise after a week indoors.'

Jagger relished the prospect of the excursion. He had gone to a great deal of trouble to choose a marquise solitaire ring, of at least approximately the right size, and in his imagination he envisaged a country walk in fine weather followed by tea at Beckford as the ideal context for its presentation. He was right. The day dawned bright, if a little cool because of a fresh north-easterly breeze, and Helen and Lionel set off on their bikes, heading south to Laverton and then west to Wormington. There they left their bikes and continued on foot, each with a little rucksack in case they wished to shed a garment or two as they warmed up. Jagger gave no hint of what was on his mind. They chatted about a variety of subjects. They had not had occasion to discuss between themselves Wednesday's staff-meeting, and it was Helen who brought the subject up. She wondered whether it had done any harm to Lionel's career. He thought not. His opinion was that these men were sufficiently broad-minded and Christian not to hold it against a man, even where they thought him mistaken. She replied that it was not a question of his being right or wrong, so much as of the damage he could do to the establishment if he persisted: the Institute cared greatly about the boys in their care and for the reputation of the college, after more than 120 years of successful education. Lionel dismissed the exchange with Fr President and the subsequent turbulence as a minor disturbance, the ripples of which would soon fade. Ah, yes, she said, but did Lionel never intend to revisit the debate? He had, he told her in reply, given the matter some thought. He had assured the headmaster that he would not raise the subjects in class, with impressionable and vulnerable teenagers, but he did not think that that precluded further discussion amongst the staff. His problem was that he could not decide on the best method of approach. For the moment, no renewal of the topics could hope to succeed while feelings ran so high. In time to come, perhaps during the autumn term, he might persuade the president to set aside a Wednesday staff-meeting with just the one item on the agenda. He, Jagger, could prepare a short paper, to be submitted to all the staff beforehand. A reasoned debate could then take place. He supposed that members of staff violently opposed to the very idea of debating educational theory might be allowed to stay away. It was all very conjectural at this stage, and he refused to think about it any further until nearer the time. In the meantime, he was going to enjoy the final days of term and to look forward to the three-week Easter break. This led Helen and Lionel to outline their plans for Easter. If his offer of an engagement was accepted, Lionel hoped that part, if not most, of the Easter holidays would be spent in Helen's company; but he refrained from mentioning the subject most on his mind.

Just past Dumbleton, the walkers took the track over the northern shoulder of Alderton Hill and proceeded down to Alderton, a pretty village predating the Doomsday Book (but unfortunately not in Worcestershire!), with a church dedicated to St Margaret of Antioch - a probably apocryphal saint whose cultus was seemingly brought back from the east by returning crusaders (and the dedicatee of St Margaret's, Westminster, no less!). From there a brisk two-mile walk brought them into the centre of Beckford and the Silk-Worm Tea-Rooms. There were quite a few people taking tea, but Helen and Lionel chose a table a little apart, and after the delivery of tea and hot tea-cakes, Lionel proposed. Let your chronicler not dwell on the scene; let your imagination run riot. Lionel Jagger used the sweetest phrases he could command – with not a Shakespeare quotation in sight – produced the ring and declared his undying love. She blushed prettily, stammered a suitable response and slipped the ring on her finger. A sharp-eyed local – a lady of middle-age, in tweeds and a floral hat, bearing the words Country-Dweller on her rosy cheeks – witnessed the occurrence, deduced the existence of a mutual romantic attachment and broke into heartfelt applause. This was quickly taken up by the other customers, and a cheer rose above the tea-cups. It was all very satisfactory and surpassed even Lionel's expectations. The two walked back to Wormington in a glow of reciprocal affection, holding hands whenever the path permitted. Lionel, thinking it better not to spoil the occasion by prolonging it artificially, much as his heart dictated otherwise, kissed Helen goodbye at her gate and walked light-footedly to his own bachelor cottage at Mincliffe, running over the afternoon's events and dreaming of the future. The fulfilment of his dreams, unfortunately, went awry – terminally awry, as I shall now tell you.

Human life evinces countless cases of the failure of plans and dreams. The future is not ours; other powers are at work in the weft and warp of existence. Are these powers benign? St Paul thought so: 'All things work together for good,' he writes, 'to those who love God' (if that is what he said: the manuscript tradition is uncertain!). Others are less sure. That 'heathen pessimist' (as he has, I think unjustly, been called), Omar Khayyám, wrote, did he not:

After a momentary silence spake
Some vessel of a more ungainly shape,
'They sneer at me for leaning all awry:
What! did the hand then of the Potter shake?'

I suppose this is an easy way to blame all the universe's faults on the creator and absolve humankind from its errors. There is no doubt, however, that humans do not yet control the universe.

The following morning, Sunday, Jagger was surprised by a knock at his door, quite early. It was Helen, sobbing, not wearing her engagement ring but holding it in her hand. Jagger looked at her with astonishment.

'What on earth?' he expostulated. 'For heaven's sake, come in, Helen, come in!'

'I won't, I can't,' she cried. 'I'm so sorry: here's your ring.' She thrust it into his hands and, turning, fled down the path in the direction of her own house, one hand to her face, to stifle the sobs. Jagger, astounded beyond measure, hurried after her.

'Helen, Helen,' he shouted. 'What on earth's the matter?' He caught up with her at her door.

'Helen, please tell me what the matter is. Can I help? What's wrong?' The pair stood there, facing each other, she with the tears of misery streaming down her face, he with a look of complete bewilderment.

'Jed's come back,' she cried. 'I can't go through with our engagement. I can't think straight. Oh, why does it all have to happen just now?'

'Look, can I come in a minute?' Jagger asked. 'I need to know more. Where's Jed now?' Helen entered the house, Jagger following in her wake. She threw herself on the sofa in her front room, crying.

'Oh, Lionel, I'm so sorry. I don't know what to say to you.' When she had calmed down a bit, she told Jagger what had happened. After her return the previous afternoon, she was tired and decided to relax with a cup of tea before thinking about a spot of supper. She was quietly reading in her chair when a ring of the doorbell roused her. There, on the doorstep, looking almost as young as when she had last seen him, stood Jed Matthews, hat in hand, a big smile on his face. She was so stunned that she stood there, gaping, until he asked whether he might come in. Before reacting, as she faced him on the doorstep - slim, handsome, weather-brown Jed, his face lit in a well-remembered grin, his eyes shining with a smile - all her old feelings for him came flooding back in an uncontrollable tide of love and affection. She could not help herself. She forgot Jagger. She forgot the afternoon's events and her engagement. Her childhood and adolescence welled up irresistibly, and she threw her arms round her newly rediscovered lover. They stood there, clasped in a tight embrace, seven years of separation shed in an instant. As soon as they had recovered from this first meeting and sat down inside, Helen realised how, in the first flood of emotion, she had betrayed Jagger. She drew the ring from her finger and promised herself that she would explain to her fiancé; he was a good man, he would understand.

Jed had left Worcester before Helen's return at the conclusion of her first term up at Nottingham, unsure whether, in her presence, he had the courage to say goodbye. The urge to try out his desire to retire to a lonely spot would not be gainsaid: he simply had to allow it expression if he were ever to experience peace of mind. If it did not work out, he would swallow his pride, return to Worcester like the repentant prodigal son and pick up the old threads. His work as guardian of Fladda consisted principally of protecting the important population of roseate terns from human predators. Fladda was an uninhabited island off the west coast of Mull, protected by the Inner Hebrides from some of the worst Atlantic weather, but his life was still primitive. On the other hand it was largely undisturbed. He had recently been offered a less harsh posting on an island off the coast of Wales, where the accommodation permitted a wife, where visitors were received in the summer months, and where there was enough summer work for two people. He had found out from Helen's parents where she was working and had called on her to renew their acquaintance. If she was free and willing to join him, he would be jubilant, but if not, he would understand: he had long ago renounced any claim on her. Helen and Jed sat talking long into the night, discussing the new posting, the possibilities that faced them, their individual hopes for life. As they talked, Helen came to the persuasion that her life lay with Jed and the sea-birds and that the teaching of biology should, at least for the foreseeable future, be adjourned. She would hand in her notice immediately and would leave Mincliffe at the end of the academic year. Jed would have taken up his new position in mid-April, and she would join him there. She might even be able to engage in some useful research, who knows? However, Jed was due to return to Murcot on the following afternoon, to give her time to reconsider her decision if she wished.

Jagger had no words to express his stupefaction. Here, in a second, his dream was gone. It had evaporated as surely as if a great hot wind had blown it into the distant stratosphere. Helen seemed so regretful, so committed to her new future, so self-assured now that she had made her decision and been able to tell Jagger, that Jagger sat there in silence, drawn, gaunt. There was nothing he could say. Desolation swept over him. He rose uncertainly, turned his back on her and left the house.

'There are many more fish in the sea.' There are not. Some human relationships are irreplaceable. Jagger sat at home, apathetic, listless, uncertain where his future lay. He had to get through a whole term with Helen as a colleague. He had to carry on as if nothing were troubling him, in front of the boys and the staff. His mood veered viciously between grief, anger, disorientation and revolt. He sat there without eating and drinking, until he came to the decision to make a final appeal to his beloved. He wiped his face, combed his hair, pulled himself together and strode over to Helen's house. The front door being open, he went straight in, with a quick rap as he passed it. Helen and Jed were sitting hand in hand on the sofa. His caution and self-control were abandoned on the instant, and he shouted out,

'Why did you have to spoil everything, you bastard? Couldn't you have left us in peace?' He looked so threatening that Jed got up rapidly from the sofa, while Helen appealed to him to calm down.

'Lionel, Lionel, I'm so sorry,' she said, 'you know I am. Do you think I *want* to hurt you? Please understand that I've known Jed since childhood, a whole lifetime: we're made for each other.'

'So that's it, is it? Your mind's made up?'

'My mind's made up,' she said with great simplicity. 'We'll still be friends. I just can't marry you any more. Please, Lionel, please try to understand.' He was already in the hall.

'You haven't heard the end of this, Matthews,' he shouted over his shoulder as he left the house.

The last week of term would be a trial, Helen knew. She would avoid Jagger as much as she could, staying in her laboratory classroom for breaks, having lunch at home, doing her marking away from the staff-room. It was only occasionally that she would see him; and when she did, she would take an alternative route where one was possible. They would be in the same room for few occasions: the weekly briefing on the Monday morning, daily assembly, a school concert. She hoped that, at the expiration of that term and the Easter holidays, Jagger would be sufficiently reconciled to the situation not to perpetuate the tension and awkwardness of this last week of term. It would be stressful but possible. Helen and Jed had agreed that he would not again show his face at Murcot: they would meet daily in the holidays, but no further occasion would goad Jagger to words, much less to action, if it could be avoided. The chance of encountering Jagger in the corridor, however, or in the square round which the original school-building was constructed, preyed on her nerves.

The first day of the last week of term witnessed one final spat in the rumbling 'political' debate. The staff-room was busy after lunch. Teachers arrived for a final cigarette; others left to put final preparations to their afternoon classes; some settled down for a bout of marking; others came in to collect books. A small group sat round one of the tables quietly chatting. It consisted of Fr Duffin, history, Fr Hendon, bursar, Mr Smith, art, and Br Ellison, retired. In a move that some saw as deliberately provocative, although that construction, said others, could be put on it only by the malicious, Jagger brought his mug of tea over and occupied the only vacant seat in the circle. To an impartial observer, this would seem to be perfectly normal and inoffensive. As there seemed to be a pause in the conversation at this point, Jagger asked whether anyone had read Morris West's latest novel, *Harlequin*. No one had. Someone asked him what it was about.

'It's about a banker whose integrity is beyond question until he's framed for a murder by an envious rival. He then resorts to all sorts of skulduggery to save his bank, his reputation and indeed his very life.'

'Any good?'

'Not bad,' said Jagger. 'I'm not sure he's got the characterisation right, and it's rather verbose, particularly the first half. It's not up to some of his earlier stuff.'

'Hasn't West been excommunicated?' Br Ellison asked, a touch sourly.

'No, brother, you've got that a bit wrong,' Jagger replied. 'He divorced his first wife and remarried just after the war; so he's not in good odour with the Church. But that just points up the absurdity of Church law: you can commit murder, acts of terrorism, atrocities in war, incest and so on and be forgiven, whereas if you divorce and remarry, you're excluded from the sacraments for ever. To me it doesn't make any sort of sense. I mean, divorce isn't exactly in the same league of evil as rape and torture, is it?'

'Well, young man,' said Br Ellison, 'to my mind you're too free with your criticism of the Church's teaching. I'm not sure you make a colleague I'm very comfortable with, and I'm not sure I see why you bother to teach at a Catholic school.'

'I can tell you that, brother, if you really want to know. Despite all my dissatisfaction with the Church, I shouldn't consider myself anything but a Catholic, just as West always did. Maybe he couldn't receive communion, but that didn't stop him from regarding himself as a member of the Church. Because of his religious background, many of his works deal with moral and religious themes - admirably so, in my estimation: *The Devil's Advocate* and *The Shoes of the Fisherman* in particular, I suppose, but also *The Second Victory*, *Daughter of Silence* and so on.'

'Yes,' said Fr Hendon pacifically, looking round the circle of listeners. 'I suppose we've all read *The Shoes of the Fisherman* and enjoyed it.'

'Ah, but,' said Jagger, 'do you remember that sentence in chapter 2: "One does not grow old in office without some hardening of heart and will"?' Total silence greeted this quotation, so keyed up were the listeners to the atmosphere consequent on the notorious exchange of words of the previous week. The silence communicated itself to the entire room. Jagger continued to sit there, seemingly unabashed. Into the stillness Br Ellison eventually spoke.

'That's an insult to Fr President, Jagger, and you know it. That's how you meant it. You're nothing but an arrogant and impertinent little upstart with more quotations to your speech than judgement. You're a disgrace to the profession and to the Church, and I for one heartily wish the school rid of you.' He got up from his chair, looked around, perhaps to garner approval, and, gathering his cassock so that it did not sweep crockery off the table, pointedly left the room with abhorrence written on his face. Fr Hendon then spoke.

'Did you have to say that, Jagger? Wasn't it rather foolish in the circumstances? Why did you have to goad the old man?'

'I didn't "goad" him, as you put it,' Jagger replied. 'Can't one say anything in this damn place without being accused of upsetting the apple-cart?'

'Look, Jagger,' Stephen Duffin came in, 'we all know you've split up with Helen, but that's no reason to take it out on the rest of us. I think you ought to go out and apologise to Piers and make your peace. What good can quarrelling do?'

'Apologise to that old buffer? In the immortal words of king Macbeth - if quoting Shakespeare isn't now to be banned as just too clever - "Better be with the dead".'

Five

The following morning, Jagger failed to appear for his first class of the day. Following school regulations, one of the boys made his way to reception to report the absence. The fragrant Miss Busby thanked him and told him to return to his class. She telephoned through to Lionel's house; there was no answer. She telephoned through to the staff-room: had anyone seen Mr Jagger that morning? No one had. In that case, would a member of staff be kind enough to slip over to his house to see whether all was well? Mrs Crampton, who taught wind instruments and who, having had a cancellation, was sitting in the staff-room reading a newspaper, volunteered. In five minutes she was back at reception, white with shock and incoherent with stupefaction. Mr Jagger was lying in bed – with his throat cut from ear to ear. Emergency measures were immediately put in place. Matron was summoned to see to the fading Mrs Crampton. A free member of staff was sent to take Jagger's class, with the explanation that Mr Jagger had been unavoidably detained. Most importantly of all, a call was put through to the police. There was no more that the school could do. Fr Jackson, the president, Fr Bedford, the vice-president, and Fr Hendon, the bursar, awaited the arrival of the police with trepidation. What might the police not uncover? Heavens, a possible scandal!

It took Sergeant Spooner and Inspector Wickfield half-an-hour to cover the distance. They swept purposefully through the gates, drove sedately up the red-tarmacked drive and parked at the front of the school, near the familiar entrance. Wickfield and Spooner had worked on their first case together in the late winter of 1967-68: it was the Unexpected Death of Father Wilfred in Droitwich which had exercised their joint brains on that occasion. Other major triumphs were the case of the sad death of Rachel Carver in Evesham in 1970, following the murder of her father twenty years before; the case of the skeletons dug up at St Mary's Court near Great Witley in the north-west of the county – that was 1972; the deaths caused by the two-centuries old will of Joan Goode in the south of the county in 1973; the death of Mr Carrick at Grant School for girls the year before their present case; and of course the discovery of the mutilated corpse of Charles Trevelyan at Mincliffe in the autumn of 1973. This is how the school struck Wickfield and Spooner on that first visit:

> Mincliffe College was a mid-nineteenth century foundation set in fifty acres of parkland and woods a few miles out of Evesham. It was approached over a stately drive through redwoods, beeches and other native trees that permitted an obscured view of the façade. Picture, if you will, a two-storey spread in red brick. A tower stands towards the left-hand end with an ogival door, heavy and studded with broad-headed nails, and an oriel window in stone above. By the grandeur of its architecture, it proclaims itself the main entrance; but it is not. That is situated on the right-hand side, perhaps a little obscurely. For the rest, chimneys rise from the ground floor up, beyond the peak of the blue-slate roof, creating bays of mullioned windows in stone. Other chimneys rise from the roof itself. To the extreme right, in a tour-de-force of non-symmetry, the gothic front of the old school chapel rears into the sky, buttressed for added impressiveness.

Spooner was what in the olden days would have been called comely: good, clean features, an intelligent eye, a pleasant manner, and always neatly turned out. Wickfield, on the other hand, was tall and craggy, with a big nose but a kindly and humorous eye; his personal appearance seemed to matter little to him, since his clothes were generally dishevelled. The two detectives were immediately shown into the president's office, where the three senior members of staff, all known to them, were assembled. Pleasantries were exchanged, with a gravity suitable to the occasion, and the president outlined the motive for the present summons.

'I know you'll wish to make a start as soon as possible, inspector, so we shan't keep you hanging about, but just let me tell you this. Lionel Jagger is a new member of staff. He joined us in September as a replacement for Tom Hubbard, who retired. Jagger was well qualified, but what persuaded us particularly to take him on was his experience in the professional theatre. He'd become engaged to a member of the science staff, Helen Mansfield, but she apparently broke that off last week in circumstances which aren't entirely clear to me. Anyway, there has been a little awkwardness amongst the staff because of it, but nothing serious, you understand. Then this morning, when he didn't turn up for class, the receptionist, Miss Busby, asked Mrs Crampton, a peripatetic music teacher, to investigate, and there we are. We phoned you when she discovered his body at his house in the grounds.'

Dear reader, at this point I am going to interrupt my narrative to stick my neck out. As this is a so far unique, and possibly unpleasant, experience, I am inviting you to hasten on to the next paragraph if you have no wish to witness it: I am going to tell you who I think the murderer is. May I explain? I have before me a large wodge of paper on which Wickfield has scrawled his notes for this case. My task is to make sense of them for you; no easy one, I can assure you, since his handwriting is untidy and his manuscript disorderly. Let me give you an example. Take the first paragraph of this chapter. Refresh your memory. The writing is clear, concise, elegant, I hope you will agree. It gives you all the information you need to make sense of the action. However, you may not be aware that you owe it to me, not to Wickfield. This is what the inspector's notes have:

Jagger not at first class; random MOS sent to root him out; discovers body. General alarm.

In addition to this text (which I have deciphered only owing to my familiarity with his hand), there are a number of unexplained doodles and squiggles which I have to omit because I simply cannot interpret them. I warrant that you would not persevere through an entire manuscript if this was your only experience of it. Now having got this far in his – for want of a better word - manuscript, I am asking myself why Wickfield has included the preamble – the death of Higgins in Coventry. I daresay you have asked yourself the same question, alert and inquiring reader that you are. Have we come up with the same answer? My answer is that it contains the motive for Jagger's death; there can be no other reason. Now the only person in that narrative who has any cause to wish Jagger ill is Amy, the bereaved wife. You will ask yourself, as I did, how Amy knew that Jagger was responsible for her husband's death. I think you will find – and remember that it is probably fair to say, without boasting, that I have a greater insight after all these years into what passes for Wickfield's mind than virtually anyone else – that she left the theatre shortly after the men and witnessed the fight, only was too scared to intervene. Amy has now traced the killer to Mincliffe and wreaked her vengeance. Like you, I have no knowledge yet of what the rest of Wickfield's manuscript contains, but I shall be very surprised if I am wrong in my assessment of the situation. Will you therefore accept a challenge? If you have another idea and it turns out to be correct, I shall apologise unreservedly to you at the end of the book. If, on the other hand, I am right and you disagreed at this present point in the story, you undertake to buy another book in this series. I cannot be fairer than that, can I?

Wickfield and Spooner's first duty was to inspect the body, even before the scene-of-crime team had worked their magic. Jagger's cottage was a semi-detached house, built between the wars when the first lay-staff appeared at the school. There were two rooms downstairs (a sitting-room and a kitchen), and two rooms upstairs (a bedroom and a bathroom). A patch of garden at the back was neatly kept. The front-door was unlocked. Jagger lay on his back in bed, the linen of which was soaked in blood. His eyes stared vacantly upwards. There were no other signs of disturbance. His clothes lay on a chair, his shoes underneath. Apart from the macabre corpse, the house seemed peaceful. Jagger's assailant, Wickfield deduced, had entered the house unopposed, walked up the stairs, entered the bedroom, only murder on his mind. He had seized the sleeper by the hair of his head, cut his throat swiftly and then left the premises as stealthily as he had entered. Or she, of course. Mustn't forget our Amy, must we?

Thinking that nothing further was to be gained at that juncture by prolonging their visit to the cottage, Wickfield and Spooner returned to the school and sat down with the president and the other two members of the senior management team. A preliminary overview of the situation was essential.

'It's a bad business, sure enough,' hazarded the inspector. 'It's not going to look good for the school, I'm afraid, fathers. We can hope only that no member of the staff is responsible: it could well be that the seeds of the murder lie elsewhere; that could be your salvation; but let's begin with the school. Tell us about Jagger, the initial interview, his arrival and so on.'

'Well, inspector, Tom Hubbard gave in his notice in plenty of time – but we all knew anyway that he was retiring, so it was no surprise. He'd done excellent work in the school for many years. We advertised for a replacement in the usual way, got a good field of candidates, short-listed four and interviewed four. We always ask why a fellow wishes to leave his present employment and also why he wishes to join us in particular.'

'And what did Jagger say?'

'He told us he'd always intended to become a teacher, but that he'd wanted to offer an experience of live theatre that other candidates would be unlikely to match. After some years of repertory work in the provinces, he'd decided that the time was ripe to move on and that he could apply with a good conscience for a teaching post that required drama. He had a good degree from a Canadian university, which we were happy to accept, and his experience at Coventry certainly weighed heavily with us. In addition to those two things, he seemed to be extremely widely read, very personable, self-confident without being self-satisfied; and of course he's a Catholic. We came to the conclusion that he'd fit in.'

'And did he?'

'Yes, I should certainly say so. The boys seemed to like him, and that's possibly the main thing. A teacher won't get work out of the boys if they're turned off the subject because he's disagreeable. His relations with staff are a different matter, though. There was something a little superior sometimes in his manner, probably because he seemed to know more than most of us. He wasn't arrogant, exactly, but staff sometimes objected to his glib speech, spattered with obscure quotations, and his insight into all sorts of subjects where the rest of us are plodders. Do you know the nineteenth-century Italian poet Leopardi, inspector? A wonderful poet. Died aged thirty-eight: no age, is it? Cholera, you know. I remember once sitting on the same hill that had inspired his youthful poem *L'Infinito* and reciting it to myself, just where he had sat. That last line: *E il naufragar m'è dolce in questo mar*: quite marvellous. However, I digress. Well, between the ages of sixteen and nineteen, Leopardi tells us that he went through three distinct phases of creativity: erudition, beauty and truth. Jagger experienced the first but seemed to have got stuck in it! He hadn't quite made the break to beauty.'

'Have you still got his application letter?'

'Yes, surely, somewhere in the office. I'll get it for you.' The president went over to his desk, made a telephone call to someone called Belinda, presumably the school secretary, and resumed his place.

'Now,' Wickfield continued, 'can any of you shed any light at all on Jagger's death?' No one spoke. 'You mentioned earlier, father,' Wickfield said, 'some "awkwardness" amongst the staff following the collapse of Jagger's engagement to this Helen person. Can you elaborate on that?'

'I wasn't there, inspector, but Frank was.' Thus appealed to, the bursar told the two detectives about the short spat in the common-room.

'It seemed to some of us that Jagger was spoiling for a fight. He deliberately sat next to Piers Ellison, which after last week's staff meeting was a bit provocative, and began some apparently innocuous conversation about that Australian novelist Morris West. He quickly steered the conversation round so that he could come out with a quotation critical of Fr President. Piers saw red and stormed out. Stephen Duffin's opinion – history, inspector – was that Jagger was taking out on us the frustration and disappointment he felt with Helen. The whole thing took only a few minutes, but it left people uneasy. An alternative explanation is that the Jagger acted in complete innocence, and it was all Piers' fault for being ultra-sensitive and taking Jagger's remarks the wrong way. So I don't know.'

'So what happened at the staff-meeting you mentioned?'

'Oh, that was something else,' the president said, 'although that's what started it all. At the end of our monthly staff-meeting last week, I mentioned a proposed change of conditions to lay-staff contracts, and Jagger took the opportunity to discourse to us about obedience and democracy in a Christian community. I don't think most of us objected to what he said, or even to the way he said it – it was erudite and entertaining in its way - but some of us thought his intervention out of place, and in any case inappropriate in a new member of staff.'

'Well, he'd been here eight months, sir,' Wickfield objected.

'Yes, but we reckon you're new for at least two years after joining us. You can hardly get used to the place in less time than that. You don't know a school, inspector, until you know every boy.'

The conference continued, but nothing out of the ordinary emerged. Wickfield and Spooner collected Jagger's letter of application and moved to the staff-room to scrutinise it. Jagger's *curriculum vitae* ran as follows:

Lionel Fenwick Jagger.

Dob 3 March 1947. Nationality British.

- 1958-1964 Norwich School: ten 'O'-Levels, three 'A'-levels (English, history, Latin)
- 1964-1969 University of Windsor, Detroit, Ontario: masters degree in English with Drama. Lancers Basketball (men's team 1968, 1969). Amnesty International. Badminton Club. Debating Society. Christian Fellowship. Call and Response Theatre.
- 1969-1972 Belgrade Theatre, Coventry: member of the repertory company
- 1972-1974 Bishop Ullathorne School, Coventry: teacher of English

Interests: international sport, reading (history, philosophy, religion etc), canoeing, philately, music.

Achievements of which I am particularly proud: academic prizes at secondary school (seven in all); 1st XI (two years); the Helena M.Coyle BA Prize in English 1965; Adele Wiseman Poetry Award, 1966; feature in the *Coventry Evening Telegraph*, 3 December 1971.

So far, so good: for a relatively young man, Jagger had achieved well. His accompanying letter read as follows:

> Dear Fr President
>
> Please find attached my cv in connection with the post of Head of English at Mincliffe recently advertised. I believe I can bring to this post a wide range of qualities which will enable me to make a very positive contribution to the school.
>
> In the first place, I am well qualified, with a masters degree in English, which has the additional advantage of emphasising drama - a particular area of focus at Mincliffe, according to your advertisement. In the second place, I would come to Mincliffe with valuable experience in professional theatre, gleaned at a new and prestigious provincial repertory company, and with teaching experience at a Catholic school. In the third place, I can offer games coaching and supervision. In the fourth place, I believe that my personal qualities will commend me to you as a teacher: I am reliable, confident, articulate, patient and efficient. I have a wide range of interests which enables me to get on with a broad spectrum of pupils, colleagues and friends. I take a great interest in my work, and in the last two years I have put a lot of effort into preparing the set texts for examination candidates.
>
> In short, I can bring a perfect balance between youth and experience which makes me, I believe, an ideal candidate for the post of Head of English with Drama at Mincliffe. I should be very happy to attend for interview at your convenience.
>
> The two personal referees I should like to nominate are:
>
> Rev. Thomas Croker
> All Souls Presbytery
> Kingsland Avenue
> Earlsdon
> COVENTRY CV5 8DX
>
> Mark Crudson Esq
> Poste Restante

Stivichall
COVENTRY CV3

'It certainly rings with confidence,' Wickfield commented. 'But then you'd expect that in a job application. No point in not making the most of yourself. Let's have a look at the two references.' The Reverend Thomas Croker had written this:

Lionel Jagger

Lionel has been a member of this parish for some time, and he has proved himself an active and supportive parishioner. He is a reader as part of the Sunday rota, he helps out with various parish activities, and I am considering inviting him to apply for status as an official catechist. I hear good reports of him from the headmaster of Bishop Ullathorne School, but no doubt you will be asking him specifically, as Lionel's present employer, for a professional reference.

The personal reference from Mark Crudson was slightly more fulsome. It was addressed from 3 Alpine Rise, Stivichall, Coventry CV3 7UD.

I have known Lionel for many years, ever since we were boys together at school in Norwich. I was struck straightaway by his self-confidence and the zest with which he set about his studies, as if he were determined to make his mark not just on the material but on all of us fellow-pupils as well. There was also about him a boyish innocence, ingenuousness, almost naivety, which was rather engaging. He shone in his studies and on the sports field. He made friends easily as a tolerant and agreeable companion, despite making demands on people's loyalties in the same spirit in which he pledged his. We have not met often recently, as our respective universities kept us separated by great distances, and then our jobs took us in different directions, but I retain a great respect for his personal qualities and for his social graces. (signed) Mark Crudson.

'At the moment,' the inspector continued, 'I'm not particularly concerned with Jagger's past: the seeds of his murder seem to me to be here at Mincliffe. What do you think, young sergeant?'

'I agree, sir. Anything you say, sir.'

'Come on, Spooner, no mucking about, we need some serious thought. Take me through it.'

'Right, sir, one or two points. First of all, it strikes me that cutting someone's throat is a man's way of killing – on the whole. The latest statistics I know of show that only 6% of women kill their victims this way, whereas 30% use poison, for example. Secondly, Murcot is not exactly an easy place to get to in the hours of darkness: the murderer would risk being seen on foot or in a car; that points to somebody local – I think. Thirdly, how many people would know that Jagger didn't lock his front-door at night? – except that that is something we need to investigate. Fourthly, we've been told of tension amongst the school staff, and we may not yet have been told all of it: there could be a cauldron bubbling away unseen that would explain the murder. If the killer is an outsider, we shall have to ask why he struck at this particular time, to coincide with an internal clash of views at the college. Fifthly, since nothing in the house has been disturbed, that we can tell, theft wasn't the motive.'

'Not bad, sergeant. So where do we start?'

'With respect, sir, we've already started – or have we been wasting our time for the last two hours?'

'No, you're right. What I really meant was, where do we go from here? I favour a word with Br Ellison, if he's available.'

Six

The president put a small room on the first floor at the disposal of the investigating team: more of a space than a room, if the truth be told, but adequate for their needs. They required merely a place to sit and interview in private. There was no need for comfort, much less luxury (luxury at a boys' public school? the heavens forfend!). Br Ellison did not strike the detectives as malevolent or defensive. Wickfield thought, not for the first time, that a life 'in religion' endowed a man - or a woman, he supposed, but with nuns he was much less familiar - with a certain placidity of temperament besides gravity of purpose. He was a rather fleshy individual, with heavy features, an immobile face and grizzled hair. He lowered his considerable weight carefully into the 'guest' chair.

'Well, now, brother,' Wickfield began benignly, 'we've heard that you had a difference of opinion with the late Lionel Jagger yesterday and wondered whether you'd tell us a bit more about it.'

'So I'm a suspect for his murder, am I?' the other grumbled. 'Didn't like the bloke, but I certainly didn't murder him, so you're wasting your time.'

'No, we're not suggesting you did, but you'll understand that we're trying to build up a picture of how he fitted into the establishment. You're someone not likely, by all accounts, to fob us off with a bland sketch that wouldn't get us very far.' He could see that his words had struck home.

'I disliked the man intensely, inspector: nothing but a conceited little pup. He came waltzing in here, dismissing us all as stuffed shirts and our years of experience as irrelevant, and then had the effrontery to preach to us on educational theory! He should have had the modesty to settle in, to imbibe our methods and the culture which has made us so successful, before opening his great mouth in disparagement. Just too big for his boots.'

'May I ask, sir,' said Spooner, 'whether many others shared your opinion, do you know?'

'Yes, quite a few amongst the members of the Institute. Our founder was a considerable theorist, sergeant, with clear ideas on how children learn and the sort of environment that encourages Christian virtue and intellectual growth. He was no half-baked amateur, and no charlatan either. Of course, we need to adapt and adjust his philosophy in the light of changing society. For example, one day we may feel the need to extend to girls the education we offer at the moment only to boys, but what we certainly don't need is some insignificant little nonentity, still wet behind the ears, to tell us our business.'

'Did you get the impression that he knew what he was talking about? Was it just his forwardness you objected to?'

'The whole man was obnoxious, inspector. Look, I daresay the pupils liked him, but then they're not old enough to discern high quality from dross. I daresay he was widely read, clever – much *too* clever – with a certain superficial charm, but we of the Institute are not looking for surface glitter. You see, what he lacked was judgement, gravitas. With him everything was just too slick; he had to be smart. Now if I'd been in his shoes, just starting out on a new job, I'd have kept my mouth shut; I'd have taken time to assess the community of which I was now a part, to weigh its strengths and perhaps identify its weaknesses. There would have been time enough to mention possible modifications later, when I'd settled in and felt I'd understood the principles behind the system. What does Jagger do instead? He swans in and blurts out a whole lot of mumbo-jumbo dressed up as learning, when all it is is a few quotations thrown haphazardly together, but like the pieces of Paley's watch, they'll never make a viable theory. He stood for spread, not depth, and that's why I took against the man.'

'If you'd been the president, brother,' Spooner asked, 'how would you have dealt with him?'

'Oh, well, the president dealt with him in his own way, I understand, and effectively too. I'd have done the same: told him to shut up and keep his counsel until he was older and wiser.'

'I'm sorry to persist, brother,' Wickfield added, 'but doesn't a school also need youth and energy?'

'We have that in abundance, inspector. We're not all as worn out and cynical as I am. Look about you at the other staff. In any case, there's a certain perennial youth in the Institute, which you will begin to appreciate, I hope, if you spend more time with us.'

'You took against Jagger, brother, to use your own phrase. Do you think he was actually in danger of damaging Mincliffe and what it stood for?'

'Who knows where his indiscretions might have led? The president was right to slap him down right at the beginning, but my fear is that he would have proved incorrigible and irrepressible, and that there was no cure but dismissal.'

'Would dismissal have been an option?'

'Oh, yes, all new lay staff work a year's probation. He could have been fired at the end of the year, if not before.'

'Have you any ideas about who might wish to have murdered Mr Jagger? It does seem a fairly drastic way of silencing a man.'

'That's your answer, inspector. No member of the Institute would have bothered murdering him, knowing that he could be got rid of bloodlessly, if you'll pardon the word, in the normal course of events. He'd have been pushed out discreetly and given a good reference so as not to prejudice his chances of a satisfactory billet elsewhere. Here wasn't the place for him, but murder just wasn't an option.'

'Yes, all that seems fairly clear, brother, but we did get the impression that feelings in the common-room were running quite high.'

'High, maybe, inspector, but not sky-high.'

Wickfield thought that next on the agenda should be a conversation with Miss Helen Mansfield, the ex-fiancée. They asked whether she would mind a short interview after her lunch. She told them that the vice-president had given her permission not to attend afternoon school, as she was coping badly and her morning classes had already suffered from her lack of attention; time was therefore her own, although she could not promise to be very coherent. Wickfield, Spooner and Miss Mansfield accordingly met in the interview-space upstairs just as the school were returning to afternoon class or, in some cases, clearly, to games. Miss Mansfield was a neat person, well manicured, with fine skin and a small round face, out of which shone two vivid, blue eyes. You may remember the 'Dialogue' in Fielding's *Joseph Andrews* between the Revd Mr Abraham Adams and the landlord of an unnamed inn about the possibility of reading a person's character from his face. The landlord tells Mr Adams that he is too widely travelled and too experienced a man to give any credence to a person's countenance. 'I would look there perhaps,' he declares, 'to see whether a man had had the small-pox, but for nothing else!' In reply the parson tells his host that 'nature generally imprints such a portraiture of the mind in the countenance, that a skilful physiognomist will rarely be deceived'. You may remember also that, despite becoming rather warm, the debate reaches no agreement on the point. Without pretending to decide the issue here, I can tell you that Wickfield read candour in Miss Mansfield's face. She had been weeping. Wickfield adopted his most avuncular manner.

'Miss Mansfield,' he began, 'we shan't keep you long, but what you have to say may be important, and we appreciate your agreeing to speak to us at this time. Please tell us all you know about Lionel Jagger and about the events of recent days in particular.'

'I don't know anything that could explain his death, inspector,' she whimpered from behind a handkerchief. 'I mean, both his parents are dead; I don't know of any brothers or sisters. We were engaged for only a matter of hours. Oh, dear, it's all so dreadful,' she burst out, as the tears rolled copiously down her cheeks. Well, dear reader, you would not thank me for reproducing the tears and sobs and cries that punctuated Miss Mansfield's testimony, so this, in plain, undisturbed English, is what she had to say.

'I met Lionel here, at Mincliffe. I'd been here two years, he was new. We began to go out together in the autumn: you know, a meal out here, a film there, the usual things. We were in a sense complimentary rather than similar: I'm a scientist, he's – he was - an arts person; I'm not particularly outgoing or self-confident, he was; my interests are quite narrow, his were wide; and so on. I liked him because of his cheeriness and intelligence and poise. Perhaps his acting had given him the sort of assurance which is essential on stage but which also has a useful social function in real life. He got on with the boys, partly because he was full of little stories and snatches of humorous verse; and of course he knew his stuff. How sincere was he in his religion? Hard to tell. The trouble with Lionel was that you couldn't gauge the depth of his feeling, so much of him was on the surface: clever words, flowery speech, lots of allusions and references which set up ever-expanding resonances, but you never knew how sincere he was, deep down. I mean, take that famous staff-meeting last week. I asked him about it directly, but he shrugged it off as a minor ripple. I think he enjoyed the exposure and pseudo-importance the exchange momentarily gave him, and there's no doubt in my mind that he would have looked for other opportunities to bring education policy up in conversation, not so much, possibly, because of the subject's intrinsic worth as because of the prominence into which his theories, which were clearly new to his audience, projected him. He liked to fly kites: let me put it that way, briefly. But you asked me specifically about his religion. I have answered that, I think, but in a roundabout way. His understanding of Christianity was, I think, very good for a layman, but then so much of Christianity is external - the trappings of worship, the visible hierarchy, the churches and cathedrals - because of the weight it puts on the bodily and the material. What store Lionel put by the inner, hidden relationship with God I'm not sure. We never really spoke about it.

'His politics? Well, now, that's an interesting one, inspector. We had several discussions on political matters, on the theory of how a humane society should be organised. He acknowledged that Athenian democracy was inadequate, for a whole number of reasons, but democracy itself, he said, if we could only elaborate a satisfactory version of it, was the ideal. In that he was right-wing. On the other hand, we didn't want a society of individuals in which the weakest sunk to the bottom. In advocating cooperation and solidarity as the key concepts, he was left-wing. On the whole, party politics left him cold. Politicians squabbled publicly and viciously, while all the time, under cover of their social consequence, they were busy-busy feathering their own nests. It was his belief in the value of democracy which set him at loggerheads with a society like the Institute, where so much emphasis is placed on traditional values and on obedience as a guarantee of stability and good order. He had a lot of ideas, one of them being that you could apply secular political theory to religious institutions. He quoted Flecker to me. In *Hassan*, he told me, a courtier comments that Ishak is preaching "sheer heresy". Flecker puts the following reply into Ishak's mouth: "Then a plague on your religion!" And I think that encapsulates Lionel's view of both politics and religion: tradition was valuable only in so far as it still served its purpose; constant vigilance was required. The trouble was, it was difficult, if not impossible, to influence policy and decision-making from outside an institution: one had to belong, to beaver away for change from within. That's why Lionel was happy to belong to the Catholic Church in general, to a religious school like Mincliffe in particular; but is membership of a body with the sole, or at least principal, view of revolutionising it really membership, and not a sort of cunning method of attack that expresses disdain for its present form?

'His family and his past? I really don't know. All he told me was that he went to school in Norwich and then on to a Canadian university, where he read English with drama. I hadn't had a chance to meet his family – I don't even know where they are now; I don't know anything about brothers and sisters. You might think that a bit peculiar when I had agreed to marry him, but in a sense the past is precisely that - past: it's the present that matters. I was attracted to Lionel as he was in the here-and-now. He could have been the son of dipsomaniacal flat-earthers or members of the Bathing in the North Sea on New Year's Day Society; he could have rolled down Snowdon in a barrel, moonlighted by swallowing flaming torches or committed murder, it wouldn't have mattered. I was going to marry the Lionel I had come to admire and love.

'Did he ever mention enemies or suggest that his life might be in danger? No, he didn't, and I don't think I'd have believed him if he had. You see, he always gave me the impression of being in control of his own life. He wasn't the sort of person to be easily pushed about. If his life had been in danger, he'd have confronted the danger without fear, or he'd have dealt with it once for all. Physically he was well-built and strong, and I think people would have thought twice about taking him on. As regards any hostility from members of the Institute, he knew he wasn't very popular at the moment, but he had too high a regard for the priests and brothers to fear any physical harm from that direction. In any case, his first term and a half at the school were smooth and free of all incident; I think he commended himself to the authorities as an asset to the school. Oh, no, inspector, I think you can put any thought that the Institute might harbour a murderer in its bosom right out of your mind. Friends? No idea. He certainly didn't mention anyone in particular to me. You see, there again, inspector, he gave the impression of self-sufficiency. Of course, everyone needs friends, and Lionel protested that he needed me, but he didn't inhabit a world where he was dependent on others: he went his own way, confident that his own ideas and his own company were in the end sufficient.

'Could the abrupt termination of his engagement have anything to do with his death? Well, I don't see how, inspector. It's true that it wasn't a pleasant occurrence. I've asked myself a hundred times whether I could or should have acted differently. It's also true that Lionel took it badly. He threatened Jed with reprisals. His exact words? "You haven't heard the end of this, Matthews," but if you think that means that Jed had anything to do with it, think again, inspector. It's out of the question. In any case, Jed is back in Worcester with his family and nowhere near Murcot.'

The long interview came to an end: long, not because the words spoken took up a huge amount of time, but because the speaker paused often to cry and give vent to her emotions. Wickfield confided in his junior that he was beginning to build up a rounded picture of the dead man, and that that, while not being a solution of the murder in itself, was an important beginning. He was also convinced that Helen Mansfield was a trustworthy witness. At the same time, he was not going to take at its face value her unsupported asseveration that Jed Matthews was innocent of all evil intention in Jagger's regard. If Matthews regarded Jagger as a permanent threat, who knows of what violence he might not be capable? What if the two men had met on the Monday night, unknown to the woman over whom they had quarrelled? It was clear that a frank interview with Mr Matthews was urgently required.

Taking from Helen particulars of Jed Matthews' present whereabouts, the two detectives returned to Worcester and visited a house in Penhill Crescent in the western suburbs. Helen had clearly telephoned through to warn him of their impending call, as he evinced not the slightest surprise at their impressive appearance on his doorstep. Tall and slim and weather-beaten, he gave out an air of easy strength. Could this man have murdered a victim as he slept? Would he not rather have defeated him in open combat? He led the pair through to the living-room, where tea was offered and accepted.

'We're interested in the events of the weekend, sir,' Spooner said, 'as you will have guessed, and of last night. Helen – Miss Mansfield – will have told you that Lionel Jagger's body was found at his home this morning; his throat had been cut. We'd like to know where you were last night, sir.'

'Where I was last night?' exclaimed Matthews. 'You can't think I had anything to do with it?''

'We'd rather not think that, of course, but perhaps you'd humour us none the less.'

'I was here all evening with my parents, and then I went to bed.'

'I see. And you slept soundly all through the night and awoke this morning to enjoy a hearty breakfast.' Wickfield did not agree with the tone of this comment, but he would not mention it to his junior until later.

'I didn't sleep well at all, sergeant, if you must know: I've got a lot on my mind.'

'Tell us about what you've got on your mind, sir.'

'I don't know how much you know from Helen, but I got back to Worcester at the end of last week and saw her out at Murcot on the Saturday evening. She agreed to join me in my new job in Wales, as soon as the school year was over: she needed to work her notice. Then on Sunday our quiet conversation was violently interrupted by Jagger, who stormed in without so much as a by-your-leave. When he saw that Helen's mind was made up, he threatened me.'

'With violence?'

'No, not exactly, he just said that I hadn't heard the end of it.'

'What do you think he meant by that?'

'Heaven knows, sergeant. I don't see what he could have done. After all, Helen and I are grown-ups, quite able to make up our own minds about things. I felt a bit sorry for him, and I can understand his disappointment, but really, these things happen. That's life.'

'Now what's been going on in my mind, sir, is this. You were frightened that Jagger would cause trouble for you, so, to give you security, you pre-empted any action on his part with action of your own: you made sure he couldn't hurt you in the future.'

'This is complete nonsense, sergeant, and you've no right to throw out wild accusations like that.'

'Can you prove you were in this house all night, sir?'

'No, I probably can't, but I don't have to.'

'You do, I'm afraid. You see, we need everyone concerned in this affair to account for his movements last night.'

'Look, I came up to bed at, I don't know exactly, probably eleven o'clock - a little time after my parents, anyway - tossed and turned for a couple of hours, then finally dozed off in the early hours. I awoke at seven this morning, or thereabouts, and that's it. There's nothing else to tell, and if you're not satisfied, I can't help it. No, wait a minute, there was something. I heard my mother get up in the night, and my father shouted out from the bedroom, after a time, something like, "You all right, dear?" I looked at my clock, and it said 3.17 - the seventeenth day of March, you see, sergeant, date as well as the time of day.'

'Well, thank you for your time, sir. We'll leave it at that for the moment, but we may have to speak to you again. When do you leave for Wales?'

'Saturday. Don't worry, I can leave you an address and a phone number, and there's no quick escape from Skokholm. You can catch up with me if you want me, but you'll be wasting your time.'

Wickfield was dissatisfied with this interview. It had turned prickly, without apparent need. On the other hand, when he asked himself how he might have conducted it himself, he was not sure he had an answer. Gaining people's confidence and goodwill was undoubtedly a skill - it required a particularly generous and tolerant frame of mind - but there were undoubtedly times when something a little less dainty was required. Probably no harm was done.

Seven

Opining that the investigation would have to reach just a little further back into Jagger's past than the immediate few days and weeks preceding his murder, Wickfield turned his attention to the references that the school had received concerning Jagger's suitability for the post of head of English at Mincliffe. The following morning, therefore, they travelled to Coventry, where they met Fr Thomas Croker in his presbytery. It was seven years since they had needed to interview a clergyman at his residence, in the case of the Unexpected Death of Father Wilfred in Droitwich. In a marginal note, Wickfield hopes that the clergy will forgive him for suggesting that what is needed is not priests - supposed mediators between an all-gracious God who, on their own admission, meets humans where they are, and the humans he is said to have created - but ministers of the Word trained in the scriptures. That is a debate for another forum, however, he says. (I sincerely hope we are spared that in the present narrative!) Fr Croker was in his mid-forties, short and already spreading in his middle regions. Jagger's murder came as a complete surprise to him; the priest expressed his regret.

'A good chap,' he said. 'What a sad end!' When he asked for, and had been furnished with, further details, the inspector asked him how well he knew the man.

'Pretty well, I think,' Fr Croker said. 'I know we're a big parish, with six full Masses on a Sunday, but some of the parishioners are more active than others, and Lionel was one of those. He always struck me as a nice bloke, and the school spoke well of him, but, when all's said and done, how well can one human being ever know another?'

'Was there any sort of trouble or antagonism that could explain his murder?'

'Oh, no, inspector, nothing like that at all. He was with us only for a couple of years, but nothing in that time could have persuaded anyone to want to kill him. Heavens, inspector, what an idea!'

'Would you say he was a model Catholic?'

'An odd question, inspector: what is a "model Catholic"? Well, to all appearances his life was irreproachable. I never heard a whisper against his morals. As I told the head of Mincliffe in my reference, Lionel took an active part in the life of the parish, which surely bespeaks a considerable level of commitment and sincerity. In any case, the school would soon have spotted anything untoward, I should have thought: a drink problem, or women, or gambling, that sort of thing. No, all in all, Jagger was everything you could have wished for in a parishioner. I hoped he would meet a nice girl and get married, but that wasn't really my business, was it?'

While they were in the neighbourhood, Wickfield and Spooner moved on to Bishop Ullathorne School, where the headmaster, Mr Ernest Williams, would be happy to spare them a few minutes, five at most. His silver hair and large ears lay flat to his skull. Unruly eyebrows and horn-rimmed spectacles framed clear brown eyes. A tall forehead, a broad nose and a generous mouth completed the physiognomy. Mr Williams, at fifty, presented to the world a benign and homely face.

'Murdered, you say: dear, oh, dear! Whatever next? Such a nice boy, too.'

'He was with you for two years, we understand, Mr Williams. In that time was there any incident, anything at all, which might have given rise to a vendetta?'

'No, no, inspector, Lionel was a perfectly placid and easy-going individual. His theories could be a little strange, but then people's reaction was to take no notice.'

'Strange: in what way?'

'He labelled himself a "democrat", and he loaded the word with more meaning than a political commentator would give it. You see, he approached the concept not from a political or philosophical point of view, but from a religious point of view, which gave a new twist to it.'

'Could you explain, sir?'

'Yes, inspector, but this is going to take me over your allotted five minutes!' He smiled, however, as he said this. 'Jagger was always denouncing this or that writer for statements made critical of the *polloi*. So, for example, one day it would be John Stuart Mill. "Do you know what Mill has the audacity to say in his essay *On Liberty*?" he'd come out with in the staff-room. "He dismisses the public as 'that miscellaneous collection of a few wise and many foolish individuals'. Now how can we take such a theorist seriously?" Another day it might be John Toland. "I've just been reading Toland's *Pantheisticon* of 1720," he'd say. "What rubbish! Here, listen to this!" he'd continue, whipping out his note-book. "'We shall be in Safety,' Toland writes, 'if we separate ourselves from the Multitude; for the Multitude is a Proof of what is worst.'" On another occasion, I remember, he quoted Pseudo-Phoclydes. I ask you! Perhaps it was by way of oneupmanship: Jagger was partial to a bit of that. Anyway, Pseudo-Phoclydes apparently expressed the lapidary opinion, "Don't trust the people; the mob is fickle". And so on. On another day it might be Dr Johnson, or Dean Inge, or Carl Jung, or Karl Marx, or José Ortega y Gasset: someone different virtually every day. Jagger's reading was prodigious, I'll give him that. He was particularly disappointed in Jung, I remember. "What does Jung think he's doing, excoriating the masses?" he said one day to anyone who would listen. "He knows better than that; and yet in his *Psychology and Alchemy* he calls the masses 'blind brutes'! That's a terrible opinion for an intelligent man to hold." Alternatively, he'd praise writers who upheld the claims and virtues of the multitude. In a single morning's break, he lined up, if memory serves me, Pope Nicholas I, Newman, Conan Doyle, Kierkegaard and St Paul!'

'But he had constructive ideas of his own?' Wickfield asked.

'Oh, yes, that's the point of what I'm trying to tell you, but I confess his ideas were somewhat above people's heads.'

'We'd be interested to hear the gist of them – wouldn't we, sergeant?'

'Er, yes, certainly, sir.'

'Well, in so far as I remember them, gentlemen, they hinged on the empowerment he claimed was accorded by the sacraments of baptism and confirmation. He appealed to Sir Thomas More's *Utopia* as a forerunner of his own ideas. In *Utopia*, it seems, the people are – or, I suppose, would be, if utopia could ever be established – so "instruct and institute" that there's no need of "attorneys, proctors and sergeants of the laws" – and so say all of us. Jagger went back to the patristic and mediaeval theology of confirmation to argue that baptism and confirmation make no sense if they don't empower the citizen to take charge of his or her own society, at the appropriate level. So he'd quote St Ambrose to the effect that confirmation is the "perfection of Christian membership" and argue from that that "perfection" implies placing responsibility for Christian society firmly in the hands of the individual. Or he'd refer to Peter Lombard's *Sentences*. "If the Lombard," he'd pontificate, "argues that the result of receiving the Holy Spirit at confirmation is 'vigorous action', what sense does it make if all political activity is denied the recipient?" His argument was, if I understood it correctly, that the confirmed Christian is equipped to take his destiny in his own hands and to determine the life of the Church. In the secular forum, suffrage has exactly the same effect – or so Jagger said." Williams smiled indulgently.

'And what did he have to say about those who are happy to delegate their "vigorous action" to a political or clerical elite?'

'I can't remember in detail, but I suppose he would have argued that that was their choice but that they could not then complain when arrangements were made not to their liking. No, wait a minute, I think I'm wrong there, because there was a corollary to his thesis. You see, according to Jagger, if I understood him correctly, proper democracy is possible only in a Christian society. He was totally against any sort of Calvinist theocracy: that's not what he meant at all, he said – except that I now forget what he did mean! I remember this, though: in his version of democracy, priesthood was out! It was absurd to think that the baptised and confirmed Christian needed any mediator between himself and God. If priests were not required, it made no sense then to elect delegates to take their place. The trouble with true democracy, Jagger argued, was that, because it depended on goodwill, it was vulnerable to evil; only in a Christian society was there sufficient divine power to guard against evil. You could have a secular democracy, but then you had to have the most elaborate safeguards against self-seeking, venality, fraud, nepotism and so forth, and even then ... But no, sorry, can't really help you further: I'm just bumbling.'

'You make it sound like a little gentle philosophising in the staff-room, sir,' commented Wickfield, 'but in fact Jagger was preaching revolution, no less.'

'I suppose you're right, inspector, but it never seemed like that, somehow. He was perhaps too young to be taken seriously.'

'And yet he moved on from here after only two years: a bit unusual, wasn't it?'

'Um, well, inspector, I had a hand there, I'm afraid.'

'A hand?'

'Well, I did suggest to Jagger that he might like to consider somewhere, er, a little more suited to his talents: a school which gave him greater scope, shall we say. I was just a little frightened, not that he was becoming tedious but that people were beginning to take notice of his madcap theories.'

'Were you under any pressure to do this? Had anyone lodged complaints? Is that what you're saying?'

'Not complaints, exactly, inspector, just a few distant rumblings, you know: nothing serious.'

'One of the governors, perhaps?' Wickfield persisted.

'Well, perhaps.'

'You're being very cagey, Mr Williams. I wish you'd be quite explicit. We can't operate in a world of shadows and innuendo.'

'OK, inspector, if you wish. One of our long-serving governors, Mrs Marinoff, did complain to me, because a member of staff had complained to her. Jagger was undermining staff morale, she protested, by working away at people's sense of unimportance and ineffectualness and introducing ideas that had been roundly condemned time and again by popes and councils. She wanted me to get rid of Jagger, but of course you can't dismiss a teacher just for having ideas. Anyhow, Jagger took my meaning, and he left. Naturally I gave him a shining reference, which I could do in all sincerity, because his work was good and the pupils he taught were well motivated. That's it, inspector. However, to accuse Mrs Marinoff of harbouring thoughts of murder – well, it's preposterous.'

'Thank you, sir. Do you know which member of staff complained to Mrs Marinoff?'

'No, she didn't tell me.'

'Can you guess?'

'No, inspector, and it would be unfair of me to do so.'

'Well, we might have to come back to you on that one, at some later stage. For the moment, thank you for your time.'

After the interview with headmaster Williams, Spooner wondered out loud whether that was a thread which merited immediate investigation. The inspector declined to act on the suggestion, for several reasons. It seemed unreasonable to him, he explained, that a member of staff of Bishop Ullathorne school, incensed by Jagger's interpretation of the notion of 'democrat', should wait until March of the following year before creeping round Worcestershire at dead of night armed with a sharp blade. It was, further, unreasonable to believe that the mere floating of 'democratic' ideas should move any but the already unhinged to murder the proponent. Finally, if the complainant had achieved his or her aim of having Jagger removed from Bishop Ullathorne, there really did seem no need to pursue the matter beyond the school's confines. No, all in all, Wickfield was inclined not to waste time on so slender a thread.

That left only Mr Mark Crudson to interview. They drove over to Alpine Rise in Stivichall (note to the unwary: this is pronounced Sty-ch[u]l!). Alpine Rise is a P-shaped development of mixed housing on the western fringes of Coventry. No.3 is the left-hand half of a pair of semi-detached houses, with a small lawn to the front and a strip of lawned garden to the rear. The area is quiet and either insufferably bourgeois or respectably middle-class, depending on your point of view. The detectives knocked, prepared to find Mr Crudson out at work but hoping to find someone in or, failing that, to speak with a neighbour who could inform them of his place of work. The door was opened by an elderly lady of stern aspect who peered at them aggressively over a pair of rimless glasses.

'If you two miscreants are selling me encyclopaedias, go away. I'll have none of you. Leave me in peace, can't you?'

'No, ma'am,' Spooner said silkily, 'we were hoping to have a word with Mr Crudson, Mr Mark Crudson.'

'Never heard of him. Now go away.' Deciding that he did not wish to see the door slammed in their faces, at least not yet, Spooner produced his badge and said firmly,

'We're the police, ma'am. We're looking for Mark Crudson.'

'I don't care who you are or who you're looking for,' came the crisp reply. 'There's no Mark Crudson here, and never has been.'

'May I ask how long you've lived here, ma'am?'

'Years and years, since way before my husband died, and that's been fifteen.' Good heavens, this termagant had had a husband?

'And your name isn't Crudson?'

'No, it isn't, and it wasn't my maiden name either. Now good morning to the pair of you.' And she added as she brought the door firmly to, 'Loafers with nothing to do but plague blameless citizens!'

Wickfield and Spooner drove into town to consult the council offices. There was only one other Crudson in Coventry, an N Crudson of 3 Hen Lane in the Keresley area in the northern suburbs (note to the unwary: Keresley is pronounced CUR-zlee or, by some, CAR-zlee! Incidentally, Coventry is always Cov- locally, never Cuv-!). Spooner wondered out loud how any confusion could have arisen: did the man not know his own address and post-code? 3 Hen Lane proved to be an almost exact counterpart to the house occupied by the aggressive widow in Styvichall: the left-hand half of a pair of semis, etc. The proprietor could not have been more different. The policemen's ring was answered by a young man in his late teens.

'Ooh, I can't do two at once,' he said, 'not at this time of day, but come in, and one of you will have to wait.'

'No, no,' Spooner said patiently, 'you misunderstand, sir. It's nothing like that. We're trying to trace a Mr Crudson, Mark Crudson.'

'Never heard of him: should I have done?' Tiring slightly of their search, Spooner said a little impatiently,

'Look, sir, are you Mark Crudson?'

'No, and I never have been. I've told you, I've never heard of him. My name's Neil. I don't know a Mark Crudson.'

'A brother, perhaps, or a cousin, even an uncle?'

'No, no and no again! Now if you've not come to see me on business, perhaps you'll excuse me,' and he closed the door.

Wickfield and Spooner returned to their car, for want of any better course of action.

'Well, sir,' Spooner said, 'what now?'

'It looks to me, sunshine, as if Jagger forged his own testimonial. There never was a Mark Crudson: just part of Jagger's scheme to get a post at Mincliffe before he's forcibly removed from Bishop Ullathorne. How many heads would bother to probe a character reference properly written and signed by a perfectly plausible referee? They simply haven't the time. Jagger couldn't forge Fr Croker's testimonial: it was probably required by the application process anyway, at a Catholic school, and there was no way of avoiding it, but I'm afraid I'm completely stumped as to why Jagger should go to the trouble of forgery. He could obviously count on Croker to come up with the goods, but didn't he have a single friend or acquaintance he could trust as a second referee?'

'Could it be, sir, that it was just easier that way? You sit down at your desk, run a short letter off on your typewriter, sign it illegibly and post it. What could be simpler?'

'Except that there's always the remotest chance you might get found out, and then what? Why run the risk?'

Kind reader, you may remember that some few pages back I engaged you in a wager which you were tolerant enough to go along with. Might I be permitted to modify its terms? I know this is a very unusual procedure, but the circumstances are unusual. At that point in the story, I bet an apology to a further book-purchase that Amy was Jagger's killer, out of revenge for her husband's death. I should now like to change that to Crudson. You see, Wickfield is transparently incompetent (but we knew that already). He's now telling Spooner that Crudson doesn't exist, that he's a creature of Jagger's warped brain, clearly having forgotten that in his own notes *he has recounted a scene, right at the beginning of this book, in which Crudson is the recipient of a fireside confidence on Jagger's part. Now it stands to reason that Crudson cannot be a real partner in conversation with Jagger at one moment, and then a figment of Jagger's imagination at another. At least, I* think *it stands to reason: I can't see Wickfield having the nous to project into real life an evening's exchange that had reality only in Jagger's head. So are we on? Crudson knew he had no proof of Jagger's part in Higgins' death with which to assail the police, but his conscience troubled him increasingly. Eventually, after a titanic inner struggle as a deeply sincere man, he determines to avenge Higgins' death himself, as an instrument of the divine justice. He drives down or cycles over to Mincliffe one night – depending on where he lives - uses his own key to gain admittance to the Jagger residence and then dispatches his victim. Right, that is my last word on the subject. I've solved the crime way before Wickfield has even begun to reach the lower slopes. The rest of our wager stands as before. Excellent! Thank you for your indulgence. No doubt we shall find out who is right in due course (but I am fairly confident of witnessing another sale of, say,* The Spider's Banquet *or* A Death Twice Avenged).

When the detectives returned to Wickfield's office in Worcester, the results of the autopsy and of a search of Jagger's house were available. The former contained no surprises. Jagger had died of a sharp wound which had severed both the jugular vein and the carotid arteries and would have died in seconds, perhaps less. The pathologist did not speculate widely on the nature of the blade responsible for this horrible wound, beyond saying that it was probably a kitchen knife, perhaps a boning knife – in any case, not serrated - wielded by a right-handed person – male or female - standing on the left of the bed employing one swift motion. The time of death was placed at half-an-hour either side of three o'clock in the morning.

The scene-of-crime team were equally unproductive. The house showed no sign of forced entry. The murderer had left no footprints on the dry, flagged path leading up to the front-door or on the carpets. Nothing in the house had been disturbed, that they could tell. They did, however, find the knife, thrown on to a small flowerbed in the front garden: a five-inch boning knife of a kind used by half the housewives (and house-husbands) of Britain; covered in blood, but without fingerprints; and they found several brown hairs lying on the counterpane. These few details added up to this, as Wickfield told his junior. The murder of Lionel Jagger was not the work of a burglar or random psychopath. The killer knew where Jagger lived, had armed himself with a kitchen knife – Jagger's own boning life lay still in its draw, and it was unlikely that a bachelor with no known interest or skill in cooking would own two – and a pair of gloves, had chosen a time of day when no one would be about in a hamlet, and a dry night that would leave no tell-tale prints. All in all, the murderer was both determined and clever, and Wickfield relished the opportunity to square up to him. If Wickfield of the Worcestershire Criminal Investigation Department could not lay him by the heels, no one could. (I'm not making that up, by the way: it's in Wickfield's notes. Such conceit is astonishing, is it not? – or perhaps not, in Wickfield's case.)

Eight

Researching Jagger's background was proving rather more problematic than the team had thought. The immediate present - his appointment to the post at Mincliffe, the contentious staff-meeting and his engagement to Helen – seemed to be infertile territory; likewise the immediate past – Bishop Ullathorne and the referees. They would have to go further back. According to his *curriculum vitae,* Jagger had spent three years as a member of the Belgrade repertory company in Coventry, and that would be the detectives' next port of call. As the first civic theatre built in Britain after the second world war, the Belgrade became a symbol of hope and rejuvenated pride in a city whose historic centre had been all but flattened. (The bombing of Coventry centre was a considerable misjudgement, but that is another story.) The modern building, opened in 1958, is not, to my way of thinking, beautiful, but then architecture and beauty seem to have been divorced for years in modern, functional, fast-moving(?) Britain. However, our story is concerned not with the architecture but with the theatrical company which used it. Wickfield and Spooner were introduced to the director, a woman who rejoiced in the name of Bets Benge, in her forties, with an elaborate hair-style and an affected manner.

'Gentlemen,' she gushed, 'do be seated.' They were in her office somewhere on the first floor, looking out over the square and the city beyond. Since Wickfield and Spooner had only the vaguest list of desiderata – a list, not to put too fine a point on it, containing one solitary item – no sophisticated preamble was required.

'Mrs Benge,' Wickfield began, 'we're looking into the life of a former member of your company who died near Evesham two days ago, and we wondered whether you could help us with a few details of his time here.'

'Oh, my dears, is that it? You should have said so beforehand. I'm quite the wrong person for you to be asking. You see, I'm new here – hardly got my head round the names of the present company, never mind past members. You just sit tight while I see whether I can find Madge, who's the person you really want. She'll be able to help.' No little time passed, and the two men were wondering whether they had perhaps, in the flurry of theatre life, been forgotten. In the end an older woman, announcing herself as Madge, appeared at the door to beckon them elsewhere.

'Can't stay here,' she explained. 'My office is much cosier. Let me get you tea while we talk. I daresay policeman get as thirsty as the rest of us, and there's nothing like a good cup of tea to tone up the spirits, is there? Just follow me, if you would.' They followed Madge down a couple of corridors and up a flight of stairs to a tiny – 'cosy' in their guide's parlance – room somewhere at the back of the theatre, where the deputy-director apparently conducted her business. She bustled next door to prepare a pot of tea and then reappeared with a small tray containing three mugs of tea, a chipped milk-jug and a cracked sugar-bowl. Having forgotten spoons, she disappeared again. The three were finally settled – not exactly in state, however one might wish to define that, but comfortably enough.

'Now, dears,' she said, 'fire away. What can I do for you?'

'It's about Lionel Jagger, ma'am.' Wickfield paused.

'Call me Madge, inspector, everybody does. I'm much more comfortable with that. Jagger, you say? Yes, I remember him. In fact, I have cause to remember him extremely well. What's he done now?'

'No, no, it's not anything he's done. The fact is, he died two days ago in somewhat suspicious circumstances, and we're just feeling our way round the affair – for a bit of background, you know.'

'Well, you've come to the right person, inspector. There's not much goes on here I don't get to hear about. You see, I've been here since the beginning – seventeen years now – and I keep my eyes open, I do.'

'You asked us what he's done now, as if he had done something before. Is that what you were implying?'

'Well, yes, but I can't tell you whether it's got anything to do with your present inquiry, can I? It might be completely irrelevant.'

'Perhaps you'd better begin at the beginning, Madge. Just tell us what you remember of Mr Jagger.'

'Lionel came to us in 1968 or 1969, can't rightly remember exactly which. He'd done a degree at some Canadian university and fancied teaching, but he wanted a bit of theatre experience first - real theatre experience, not just amateur stuff. Very sensible, in my view. Anyway, he very soon made himself at home. He got on well with people, he could act, he was keen and energetic, and we began to think that we'd got a treasure. Well, we had, I suppose, but he was the cause of our losing another valued member of the cast.'

'What happened?'

'It's quite a long story, inspector: I hope you've got time for it. Can I get you a refill, sergeant? That's a good lad: I like to see a man that likes his tea ... It was like this. When Lionel joined us, probably the most valued members of the cast was a woman called Nikki, but she preferred, and virtually always used, her stage-name, Oriana. She'd come to us straight from college, so I suppose she was twenty-one or twenty-two when she joined us. Boy, did she have some curves! That always helps in this business, you know: gets the younger men in, and they're the most difficult age-group. Nikki was good, but of course her performances needed that extra polish which comes only with experience. She worked hard to improve, I'll give her that. She kept the directors on their toes by wanting meticulous instructions, which she followed to the letter and practised over and over again. Because of her pretty looks, she was often chosen to be part of the cast, and there were muttered accusations of favouritism. You know the sort of thing you get in any closed company: mutterings like, "she wouldn't have got that part unless someone were inside her knickers" - saving your presence, gentleman.

'Now we had several young men in the cast, to take on the dashing or villainous characters: you know, the Brindsley Millers and Bosolas of the theatre world. One of these was a good-looking bloke called Dirk - Dirk Rider. He was a graduate too, and ambitious with it. He made no secret of using the Belgrade as a stepping-stone to a more glamorous career, but that was all right with us. "So-and-So cut his teeth at the Belgrade before making the big time at The West End" - that does us almost as much good as having a well-known actor permanently on the cast. The trouble with Dirk - one of the troubles with Dirk - was that he tended to sing his own praises. He regarded himself as superior to the others: he was better qualified - which I don't think he was - he had a better presence, he was going further, and so on. This was not designed to endear him to his colleagues, and one person in particular who took exception to his boasting was a chap called Malcolm Prendergast. Malcolm was a good actor, but the trouble with him was that he was socially gauche: awkward with the girls, didn't socialise very much, kept on putting his foot in it. He just wasn't easy to get on with. He was one of these people who always managed to say the wrong thing. He meant well, I'm sure, but it just never came out that way. I liked him myself, and he was always very polite to me, but I know he put some people's backs up. Malcolm took to making snide comments about Dirk's hoity-toity ways. When Dirk appeared for a rehearsal, he'd declaim, "O world! how apt the poor are to be proud" - that's *Twelfth Night*, by the way - or, "The fishermen that walk upon the beach Appear like mice" - *King Lear*, gents. And so it went on, day after day. The director was at his wits' end to bring some sort of civilised coexistence into proceedings. Once he called the two men into his office and had a go at them. "This can't go on," he told them. "We're a small team, we need to work together. We can't have you two set by the ears all the time." For a time, things quietened down; then it got to being as it was.

'Everyone was affected by it, not least our Nikki. You see, she was often playing with or against either Dirk or Malcolm. I remember one production of Shaw's *Major Barbara*. Oriana was playing Sarah, one of the daughters; her fiancé Charles Lomax was Dirk, while the arms-manufacturing father Undershaft was played by Malcolm. May I remind you of one scene?' She rose from her seat, and acted out the four parts – given the exiguous space available, with considerable expertise. 'Some of the characters are being given a tour of the armaments factory,' she went on. 'The foreman appears with Lomax. "Anything wrong, Bilton?" Undershaft asks his foreman.

> BILTON. Gentleman [*indicating Lomax*] walked into the high explosives shed and lit a cigarette, sir: that's all.
>
> UNDERSHAFT. Ah, quite so. [*Going over to Lomax*] Do you happen to remember what you did with the match?
>
> LOMAX. Oh come! I'm not a fool. I took jolly good care to blow it out before I chucked it away.
>
> BILTON. The top of it was red hot inside, sir.
>
> LOMAX. Well, suppose it was! I didn't chuck it into any of *your* messes.
>
> UNDERSHAFT. Think no more of it, Mr Lomax. By the way, would you mind lending me your matches.
>
> LOMAX. Certainly.
>
> UNDERSHAFT. Thanks. [*He pockets the matches.*]
>
> LOMAX [*lecturing to the company generally*] You know, these high explosives don't go off like gunpowder, except when they're in a gun. When they're spread loose, you can put a match to them without the least risk: they just burn quietly like a bit of paper. Did you know that, Mr Undershaft? Have you ever tried?
>
> UNDERSHAFT. Not on a large scale, Mr Lomax. Bilton will give you a sample of gun cotton when you are leaving, if you ask him. You can experiment with it at home.

SARAH. Bilton will do nothing of the sort, papa. I suppose it's your business to blow up our enemies; but you might at least stop short of blowing up poor Charles.

'Now at that point in the drama, Lomax is meant to come in with a comment to his beloved Sarah: "My ownest, there is no danger," but before he could do that – at this one performance I'm talking about – Undershaft chipped in with the completely unscripted and inauthentic words, "No, but it might be a bloody good idea if I did". There were a few laughs from the audience, but I'm not sure they understood how the sentiment might fit into the action of the play. In Dirk's dressing-room the following day was a small barrel labelled "TNT" in big letters. Malcolm denied all knowledge of how it got there; he swore he had nothing to do with it. The director said that he couldn't cancel the last few performances just because two of the actors were playing silly devils and putting the success of the play at risk, but if the two men didn't sort themselves out instanter, they'd both be given the boot. Well, that wasn't quite fair on Dirk, and I'm not sure the director would have got away with it anyway, but peace, of a kind, was reimposed.

'It was then that Lionel Jagger decided to intervene. He was new, taken on to fill Malcolm's place. Malcolm had expressed his wish to move on, you see, and the director wanted a bit of overlap. While *Major Barbara* was completing its run, other members of the company were rehearsing Pirandello's *Henry IV*: this was to be Lionel's first major role with us; but that's by the bye. As I was saying, Lionel decided to interfere in the Dirk-Malcolm business. Silly, really, because it was absolutely nothing to do with him - or so we thought. It flared up one Sunday night when some members of the cast were drinking in the Old Windmill in Spon Street. Dirk and Oriana were sitting together. Jagger walked up to them and, without any preamble, told Rider to lay off Prendergast. "You get up my nose," he told Rider, "with your insufferable loud mouth. Just stop regarding yourself as a cut above the rest of us, and then we'll all get on fine." "It's nothing to do with you, Jagger," Dirk said. "That bloke's a blot on the company, and I for one shan't be sorry to see the back of him." You see, Jagger's real reason for speaking was to put Dirk into a bad light, as if he were the one causing the trouble. What he really wanted was to get Nikki to transfer her affections to him, Jagger. Some hopes, I should say, as if Nikki hadn't already seen through Dirk's boasting, Jagger's intervention was hardly going to do the trick; but where girls are concerned, men don't always see very clearly. The upshot of all this was that Nikki handed in her notice. She told the director straight that she'd had enough of all the bickering, and even with Prendergast gone, she now had to put up with Jagger in the company. It was all too much, and she was taking herself off to start again. She was ready to try her luck in London.'

'May I ask how you know all this, Madge?' Wickfield asked.

'Everybody knew all about it, but Jagger told me his bit himself. You see, when Nikki had taken herself off, the rest of the company put the blame on him. "If you hadn't interfered," they'd tell him, "everything would be OK. Prendergast was going anyway, and Rider on his own wouldn't have caused any trouble. You've upset the apple-cart." Everybody liked Nikki, you see, and the place wasn't the same without her. Well, of course, things settled down again: they have to, when you've got a busy schedule and are rushing from one play to another.'

'Why did he tell *you*, Madge?'

'Well, ill-feeling rumbled on for quite a time after Nikki left. Jagger could feel it. Knowing I was an old hand, he came to me to ask whether he'd done something wrong. Why do the cast shun me? Why does Prendergast always give me dirty looks? What's the matter with everybody? I was sympathetic. There was already trouble without Jagger, and because I wasn't sure Nikki would have stayed anyway, I didn't blame Lionel altogether, even though he admitted coveting Nikki's affections and behaving perhaps a little inadvisedly. The director - Rik McKinnon it was then, Bets' predecessor - had a go at me: at *me*! He said I hadn't done enough to stop the trouble, and I'd done nothing to stop Nikki leaving. Well, I ask you: the nerve of the man, it fair took my breath away; but as I say, things settled down eventually. A new lead girl came - Amy - Prendergast left, then Rider left soon after, and the affair gradually slipped into the background.'

'I see,' commented Wickfield. 'All very interesting. I wonder where we can get hold of Prendergast and Rider?'

'Bets may know,' Madge answered. 'Prendergast went off to Cardiff, I think, but I don't know what happened to Rider.'

As Wickfield and Spooner made their way back to Worcester, Spooner asked his superior for his reactions to their visit to the Belgrade.

'We've been given three slender threads, young sergeant,' was the answer, 'but I'm not sure any of them is going to lead anywhere much. In fact, I'm not even sure it's worth our time pursuing them.'

'And what are the three, sir?'

'Well, obviously, McKinnon, Prendergast and Rider. All three had reason, however ill-founded, to blame Jagger for Nikki's loss to the company; but that's not a motive for *murder*, surely? Grown men may act childishly, but most realise that murder puts them into a different league altogether. They must simply swallow their distaste, anger, frustration or jealousy - whatever the emotion is eating them away inside - and get on with things. Risking a life-sentence for a moment of satisfaction is a mug's game. So I tell you what we're going to do. You'll follow up the three addresses that Mrs Benge has given us and get a signed and witnessed statement from the three men we're interested in. As I say, I'm not sanguine it'll get us anywhere, but I'll have to satisfy the DCI that we've followed up every possible lead. Ah, me, so much drudgery in this business!'

Sergeant Spooner duly obtained the three signed and witnessed statements via our police colleagues from elsewhere in the country. This is how they read.

Statement 1: Richard McKinnon. I have been asked to make a brief statement about the dispute that led Nikki Clarke, known to Coventry theatre-goers as Oriana, to leave the Belgrade Repertory Company in January 1970. The facts are these. There was a long-standing personality clash between two of the male actors, Dirk Rider and Malcolm Prendergast, both in their twenties. Neither actor, in my opinion, was easy to accommodate in the company: the former was boastful, the latter cold. It was generally understood, however, that Dirk had gained Nikki's affections, although their relationship did not, as far as I know, amount to a formal commitment. There were one or two occasions when I had to reprimand the men for unbecoming remarks or comments. This feud came to a head when Lionel Jagger, although new to the company, interfered by telling Rider to back off. Nikki took offence at being fought over like a trophy of war and tendered her resignation. I tried to argue with her, but she would have none of it: Jagger's intervention was the last straw, she said. Prendergast was going, but that would still leave Rider and Jagger fighting over her. She could not be doing with it all and wanted to lead a quiet life in the profession she had chosen and which she enjoyed. I was sorry to lose her from the cast, but I understood and accepted her sentiments. It turned out that her replacement was equally talented.

Statement 2: Malcolm Prendergast. *Why Nikki Clarke left the Belgrade Rep in January of 1970.* Here are the facts of this business, from my point of view.

Dirk Rider, one of the younger actors in the company, could act, I'll give him that, but offstage he was an insufferable bore, constantly droning on about his superiority over the rest of us. His superficial glamour dazzled poor Nikki, who wasn't really old enough to know any better, and I felt obliged occasionally to remind Rider that he was part of a company, not a one-man show. I was sad to see Nikki throwing herself away on a half-baked whelp, but she didn't seem to regard me very favourably. Then Jagger swaggered in and began to lord it over the rest of us, rivalling Rider in his self-importance. Nothing Jagger did could affect me, because I was leaving anyway, but I felt sorry for her, left at the mercy of Rider and Jagger squabbling over her like a couple of schoolboys. I wasn't close enough in the pub when Jagger had a go at Rider in front of Nikki, but I was told he called him a loud-mouth. Nikki got the impression that Jagger was now after her and told Rik that she'd had enough and was off as soon as she'd worked her notice. Who do I blame? Jagger *and* Rider. Nikki was a great loss to the company, but not to me, because she wasn't mine anyway. Her replacement, Amy, seemed able to fill her shoes quite adequately, from what I could tell.

Statement 3: Dirk Rider. *How the Belgrade lost the divine Oriana.* That bloody Jagger was a disgrace to the company: should never have been engaged. Just full of himself. Thought he had a right to push us around, and him hardly through the doors. What happened was this. Prendergast, who couldn't act to save his life, objected to Nikki and me having an informal understanding. He was just jealous, that's all. We were perfectly happy jogging along together, no pressure on either side. Prendergast kept butting his nose in: just couldn't help himself. I could handle him, however. Rik kept on telling him not to hassle me, but I didn't need Rik's help. One night, while a lot of us were enjoying a quiet drink at the Windmill, Jagger strutted over to me and told me to stop shooting my mouth off. What the hell did he know about it? It doesn't do any harm to remind the company occasionally that it contains some fine actors. Anyway, I didn't do anything – he wasn't worth it – but the next thing I know is that Nikki hands in her notice and swans off to London. Well, there's plenty more fish in the sea, so I didn't bother too much about it. However, I couldn't see myself ever getting on with Jagger, so I handed in my notice too. That's it: nothing dramatic, nothing drastic, but the whole incident left an unpleasant taste in the mouth.

Nine

Wickfield grumbled to himself, and to Spooner, that they were making no progress. There was nothing for it but to step even further back into Jagger's life in the attempt to turn up some incident that could explain the later murder. Before the theatricals, Jagger was a university student. To his university they would have to go. However, the expense of a flight for two persons being unjustified, Wickfield went on his own. He was not averse to travelling, but he hoped that the expense and time would be justified. Detroit, as you probably know, is a city divided between Canada (province of Ontario) and the United States (state of Michigan); Wickfield's business was strictly Canadian. He flew into the local airport, took a taxi to the Holiday Inn, checked in and, in view of the late hour, deferred all business until the following morning. He felt justified in spending his own money to attend a classical guitar/flute/voice recital at the University School of Music, followed by a quiet, solitary meal in a downtown pizzeria: neither of them an earth-shattering experience, but both very welcome none the less.

The following morning, he presented himself at the English Faculty off Wyandotte Street West, armed with an authorisation from the local police, and, after consultation with the receptionist, decided to ask to speak with the one of the associate professors who might have had dealings with Jagger. After the receptionist had consulted various lists, he was pointed in the direction of the room of Associate Professor Miranda Hebbert: a daunting personage (as it transpired), with a mountainous coiffure, severe horn-rimmed spectacles and a relentlessly dark suit. She proved, however, quite amenable in her reception of him.

'Yes, inspector, what can I do for you? Or, as Shakespeare has it, "'Tis not enough to help the feeble up/But to support him afterwards" – *Timon of Athens*, inspector. I'm here to support you, you know.' Wickfield, faced with a Shakespearean quotation within seconds of his introduction, quailed. He was clearly no match for this *mulier fortis*. He thought of a Shakespearean quotation of his own: 'Lady, you bereft me of all my words.' However, he managed to speak: he had to.

'Professor Hebbert,' he said, 'it's very kind of you to receive me without any notice: I appreciate it.'

'Yes, well, perhaps you'd like to get to the point.'

'Yes, of course. It's about a former student of yours, whom I'm told you tutored during his studies here: Lionel Jagger.'

'Ah, Jagger, yes, an interesting chap.'

'Interesting: in what way?'

'A voracious reader and an impressive speaker. Quite the star of the Debating Society, you know. "He was a host of debaters in himself": that's Burke, by the way. What is your interest in him, may I ask?'

'I'm sorry to have to tell you that he has been murdered.'

'Murdered? Good heavens! When?' Wickfield told her the story as briefly as he could and added that there was difficulty on identifying a motive and therefore, of course, the perpetrator. 'I really don't see how I can help,' she went on. 'I don't know anything about his murder.'

'No, of course you don't directly, professor, but I want you to cast your mind back to his time here: 1964-1969, if that helps. I'm looking for any enemies he might have made.'

'Enemies? The English department at Windsor doesn't seem a very likely battlefield, does it? We don't teach "war's glorious art" here, you know – Edward Young, inspector.'

'No, of course not, but Jagger, I've discovered, could rub people up the wrong way. At some time in his life he's made a mortal enemy, and it's my sad job to find out who it is.'

'Well, let me think. There was one incident which comes to mind, but I can't believe it made him the mortal enemy you refer to.'

'Please tell me about it.'

'I'm talking about a particular debate towards the end of Jagger's time with us – probably March 1969, something like that. The Debating Society meets once a month. It's run by the students, but under the aegis of the English department. Anyone may attend, but certain conventions are observed. For example, as you enter the hall, you are pointed towards the government or the opposition: you have no choice, in other words, about which side you speak for: "no speaking by the card, or equivocation will undo us" – *Hamlet*, inspector, if you didn't spot it – but I expect you did. Where was I? Oh, yes. The main speakers, of course, are primed beforehand, otherwise they couldn't be expected to produce any speeches worth listening to; but all other participants are expected to speak extempore for whatever side they happen to be on. You stand to speak, and nobody interrupts you while you're on your feet. When you've sat down, the Speaker will invite someone else with his or her hand up to stand and speak in their turn. It's all pretty civilised: designed to channel oratorical skills and high feelings into debate, not fisticuffs. It's also designed to enable participants to enter into the spirit and mentality of arguments with which they may have no sympathy. "Speech was given to the ordinary sort of men whereby to communicate their mind; but to wise men, whereby to conceal it" – Bishop Robert South, inspector.

'Now on this particular occasion, the motion was, This House believes that democracy may be defined as the bludgeoning of the people by the people for the people. That's Oscar Wilde, of course: "The Soul of Man under Socialism". A chap called Keuffner was speaking for the motion; Jagger was speaking against it. Keuffner, naturally, argued for Wilde's main thesis, namely, that the only form of organisation worthy of modern society is a non-property-owning, non-capitalist individualism which frees people up to live instead of accumulating things. Well, in my view, anyone defending Wilde on this point is going to have a hard job of it. Keuffner did his best, but he was no match for Jagger. Jagger began his speech with two contrasting views. He chose John Dryden first of all, proponent of the heroic couplet and other rarified poetic forms. Towards the end of his *Of Dramatic Poesy*, Dryden expresses this sentiment:

> If by the people you understand the multitude ... 'tis no matter what they think; they are sometimes in the right, sometimes in the wrong; their judgement is a mere lottery.

Jagger moved on 200 years to Matthew Arnold. I can't remember where he got this quotation from: not *Culture and Anarchy*, I fancy, which is where you might expect it, but it doesn't really matter. It went like this:

> Can it be denied, that to live in a society of equals tends in general to make a man's spirits expand and his faculties work easily and actively; while, to live in a society of superiors ... in general tends to tame the spirits and to make the play of the faculties less secure and active?

Now this was quite a clever choice on Jagger's part, because it enabled him to contrast two poets, one of whom was clearly opposed to Wilde's view, the other of whom seemed to favour it, and the audience naturally thought he would end up on Dryden's side. He didn't. He showed that Wilde – and Dryden - lacked a proper understanding of human nature.

Wilde's advocacy of individualism was based, Jagger said, on an optimistic *and unrealistic* view, whereas Arnold, despite, or perhaps because of, his cynicism, at least took the problem of human evil seriously. Jagger went on to analyse and to condemn the individualistic theories of William Godwin, whose *Enquiry Concerning Political Justice* was published in 1793 and which influenced yet another poet, the early Wordsworth.

'Then, while the audience thought they could settle down to an account of some esoteric barney between writers long since dead, Jagger suddenly switched to Tawney and Chomsky. The latter quoted the former as saying:

> Freedom, to be complete, must carry with it not merely the absence of repression but also the opportunity of self-organisation.

Jagger went on to criticise Tawney for not being Christian enough and Chomsky for being romantic. This led him to propose his own views of how society should organise itself in the light of St Paul's understanding of where humanity stood in relation to the Fall on the one hand, and to the Redemption on the other. It boiled down to arguing that no human organisation of society can be anything but a failure if its people aren't informed by a sense of inadequacy in the face of their own moral weakness. A divine potency is needed before a people can cooperate and stand shoulder to shoulder in solidarity. If you take the hallmark of a civilised society to be its willingness to care for its vulnerable members, it becomes even more obvious, in the light of our natural impatience with the handicapped, the elderly, the chronically sick and so forth, that a superhuman adhesive is required. For Jagger, however, theocracy was just as much a tyranny as atheistical communism – for example - and he expressed his dismay at attempts inspired by religion to force people to be good, and at any political theory which supposed that morality can be enforced. It was actually very interesting stuff.'

'Pardon me for interrupting you there, professor,' Wickfield said, 'but none of this constitutes a motive for murder.'

'I never said it did, inspector, but if you let me finish, you'll see what I'm getting at. Jagger's speech was clever, no doubt about it. I may have given the impression that is was long-winded and full of heavy references, but in fact he managed to convey a sense of substance and authority by however fleetingly covering a lot of ground, while at the same time keeping the tone light. You see, he punctuated his words with quotations from people everybody, or at least most people, had heard of, and yet not at such length that his speech lost its light-footedness. In other words, he gave the impression of considerable learning and research, and at the same time showed his audience that he was master of his material and had used it to go forward to something new.

'His speech was greeted with applause as he sat down. I'm not sure everyone understood his theory, but that didn't seem to matter very much in the enthusiasm of the moment. The debate wound on, but it was clear that Keuffer had lost the support of the audience - if he ever had it. Now unfortunately Jagger went beyond the demolition of the motion. His tactic at this point was perhaps inexcusable. He managed, very subtly, to imply that proponents of the motion in general, Keuffer in particular, were Wildeans, and I could see from Keuffer's face that he took that as a deadly insult. Remember, this was exactly the time of the public outcry caused by the condemnation of Everett Klippert for homosexuality and the change in the law that came about because of it. The law might be changing, but many people still favoured the pre-Trudeau stance.

'The next issue of *View* - that's the student magazine at Windsor - included a short piece by Keuffer in which he demanded an apology for what he said was an unjustified slur on his character. He outlined the circumstances of the affair, so that those who hadn't been present at the debate could be in no doubt as to the irrelevance of Jagger's innuendos and the seriousness with which Keuffer regarded the matter because of the public nature of the debate. Lo and behold, an apology duly appeared, but it was so couched that, while ostensibly expressing regret, it actually made the matter worse. Jagger included several Wildeisms, such as, "Always forgive your enemies: nothing annoys them so much", "Seriousness is the only refuge of the shallow", and "A man cannot be too careful in the choice of his enemies". No reader of the apology could fail to detect its mocking tone behind the words of contrition.'

'You seem very well informed about all this, professor.'

'That's because I chose the title of the debate, and I was in the chair. It was one of the few debates I chaired in which I witnessed brilliance, and that's why I remember it so well.'

'And have you any idea where I might get hold of this Keuffer?'

'Yes, I have: probably on campus, not very far from here.'

'What? How's that?'

'He left after his degree in political science to become research assistant to an MP in some unlikely constituency - Blackstrap in Saskatchewan, or something like that - before returning to us to do an MA. You'll find him deep in some dusty tome in the library, no doubt.'

It did not take Wickfield long to trace his quarry. After infertile visits to the Leddy Library and the political science faculty at Chrysler Hall North, he made his way to the Paul Martin Law Library on the north side of the campus, where Rudi Keuffer was quietly chewing his way through Deutsch and Merrit's *Nationalism and Social Communication: An Inquiry into the Foundations of Nationality.* The student seemed only too happy to be interrupted in his research! Keuffer led Wickfield to an annexe where talking was permitted and asked why he was wanted. He had not, to his knowledge, contravened any statute of the United Kingdom.

'A few simple questions, Mr Keuffer, that's all I need,' Wickfield said. 'I'm sorry to be interrupting your work, but I have come quite a way and really didn't want to wait longer than I had to.'

'That's all right, inspector. Fire away.' Keuffer was tall and lean, with a nose nearly as big as Wickfield's, deep-set blue eyes that bespoke intelligence, and an alert face. He can only have been in his mid- to late twenties, but his sparse brown hair made him seem rather older.

'It's about an English undergraduate you used to know here at Windsor: Lionel Jagger.'

'Yes, I know him. What's he done?'

'Well, let's just say,' Wickfield said cautiously, 'that he's come to our attention. Now I understand from Prof. Hebbert of the English department that you and Jagger were on opposite sides of a debate that took as its motion a quotation from Oscar Wilde.'

'Oh, that!' Keuffer exclaimed. 'All kids' stuff.'

'That's as may be, but Prof. Hebbert seems to think it turned pretty nasty: some story about a pseudo-apology in *View*, she told me.'

'Right, inspector, what happened was this. You're obviously not up to date, so let me tell you more about it than you seem to know. After the debate, I was furious to be smeared in public and demanded a public apology. Jagger responded with a travesty of an apology, printed in *View*, and I was so incensed I arranged to see him. I took a friend along with me and invited him to bring a friend as well. You see, unattended I feared I might be tempted to bop him on the nose, and I thought a little foursome would make things more civilised and less likely to descend into an unseemly brawl. We met one evening in the Chubby Pickle: there was Jagger, of course, me, Andy Wilmott and my friend John Iggulden. John told Jagger that his apology was laughable and, what's more, neither gentlemanly nor Christian. After some discussion, Jagger had the good grace to admit that he was at fault, and the atmosphere among us warmed as the discussion went on. Wilmott suggested eventually that Jagger and I could best make peace by collaborating in a book. Jagger was enthusiastic. He already had a title in mind – *Eutopia* – and he would be delighted to have a student of politics to collaborate with. The four of us got quite excited about the project. At the end of the evening, Jagger offered to post another apology in *View*, but I told him that wouldn't be necessary and that the offence was now water under the bridge. It was more important to be looking forward to our proposed collaboration.

'In the flurry of finals, our project vegetated. Then Jagger returned to the UK to start an acting career, while I went into politics – at a very humble level, of course, but we all have to start somewhere. That seemed to be the end of it. Then I had a letter from Lionel, posted on to me from the university, suggesting we got together to further the writing of *Eutopia*. He attached a sort of blue-print of what the book should look like. He acknowledged that many people, not least Plato, had tried to outline the perfect society, but he thought there was room for another attempt in the light of two world wars and recent social, psychological and political research. He was also keen to describe not just one society out of many, as More did, but a world society that would encompass all of humanity. He had plenty of ideas, particularly on the moral side, but he recognised that he needed a more competent contribution on the political side. I was slightly worried by his emphasis on the Christian initiatory rites as sources of social cohesion: I thought it might antagonise some readers, but he seemed amenable to discussion. Another thing I was unsure about, for the same reason, was his use of Catholic social teaching since the late nineteenth century, particularly its concepts of solidarity and subsidiarity. Anyway, after an exchange of materials by post, which occupied twelve months or more, Jagger came over here for a week last year, to further our talks face to face, and then I flew over to the UK last month, to coincide with Lionel's half-term, and we began to parcel out the various chapters or sections for which each of us was to be responsible.'

'So you were at Mincliffe just a few weeks ago?'

'Yes, but only for a few days.'

'Where did you stay?'

'At Lionel's house, of course.'

'And how did your, er, collaboration go?'

'The book is on course, inspector – well, more or less, given Lionel's present infatuation with Helen, the new love of his life, and certain difficulties we have encountered latterly. First of all, we got bogged down on a short passage Lionel had found in one of the letters of Bishop Pacian of Barcelona. Bishop who? You may well ask, inspector! Lionel had such a capacity for reading that he turned up all sorts of odd sources. Pacian, who died in about 390, was apparently a saintly bishop whose extant works consist of just three letters and a short parenaesis. In his first letter, addressed to some guy called Sympronian, if memory serves me, Pacian has these sentences:

> As you say, my lord, no one has been found in the whole world who could persuade you against what you believe ... No one could ever be convinced of the truth unless he consented to it by his own religious feeling.

I can't guarantee the precise words, but that's the gist of them. Now Lionel was for mounting an extended discussion of this point of view. After all, if you're intent on establishing the perfect society in line with Christian teaching, what do you do if some individual, or some group, doesn't agree? Can you force them? Is it practical, is it moral, to try? I argued that our book wasn't about that and that I didn't want our description of eutopia to be sidetracked into a massive argument about conscience, which is a huge subject on its own. We were on the verge of falling out over this, but because it might have been the cause of our abandoning the entire project altogether, we agreed to let it rest for the moment.

'While I'm talking in this vein, I may add that Lionel had the infuriating habit of spilling over into frivolity at the drop of a hat. I remember once he suddenly said, "Yes, we could illustrate the contrast in authoritarian styles with a reference to the tenth-century German self-styled emperor Otto." "Oh?" says I, "how's that?" "Don't you remember that lovely clerihew – a Bentley original?:

> The great emperor Otto
>
> Could not decide upon a motto.
>
> His mind wavered between
>
> *L'État c'est moi* and *Ich dien.*"

I was aghast at his lack of seriousness! He did exactly the same again when I proposed including in a footnote Lord Acton's criticism of Thomas Macaulay's essays as "flashy and superficial". "Excellent!" he said, "we could slip in another original clerihew:

> When Macaulay found Brougham

Sitting on a tomb,
He told an anxious friend
He was meditating on his latter end.

'Another bone of contention was his insistence that we include quite a lot of anti-Catholic polemic. Look at this, for instance.' He reached inside his brief-case and drew out a few sheets, which he handed over to the inspector. 'I saw no need for any of this: why alienate part of your intended readership with esoteric quotes from long-forgotten councils? However, he thought that we couldn't win over minds without showing up the weaknesses of our "opponents". So, this is a paragraph he wanted to insert:

> The New Testament is clear that Christians are of equal value in the community, all chosen by God to help bring the Kingdom to earth. Gradually, however, a clerical, and then a monastic, élite arrogated superiority to itself, with powers not merely of service and organisation but of authority. Over the many centuries since then, some members or groups of the clergy have made every effort to prevent the laity from laying the lightest finger on the levers of power. A few examples will illustrate this.
>
> - No lay person may set himself up as a teacher in matters of religion – Council of Trullo, 692, canon 64.
> - The laity are forbidden to interfere in the affairs of the Church, and, similarly, the bishops may not extend to them the Church's judicial powers – Council of Rheims, 1148, canon 5..
> - No layman may dispute about the faith in public or in private – Synod of Tarragon, 1233, canon 1.
> - The laity are forbidden to have in their possession books of theology written in the vernacular, with the exception of prayer-books – Synod of Tarragon, 1317, canon 2.
> - Lay people are not to be near the altar during divine services – Synod of Paris, 1429, canon 35.
> - The Church of God consists in her priests – St Isidore, Letter 7.

He was getting quite stubborn about this, even suggesting that the quotations be included in Latin, so that the reader could judge the accuracy of his translation themselves! I told him: "Lionel," I said, "because we're not writing a book for the general reader - a popularising account of new political and social ideas, as you seem to think – but rather a scholarly attempt at creating a new political theory for the specialist, there's no need to include all this faux scholarship."'

'And what did he say to that?'

'He said that it was a fundamental difference between us, and that we should need to clarify our respective aims before he would proceed any further. He was out to write a dashing, flamboyant, swash-buckling, roller-coaster sort of work that would impress the lay reader with its erudition and enthuse the educated public, whereas I had begun to feel that we should be looking to something weightier, more measured, which would make our name as scholars: I don't wish to be thought of as a dilettante or dabbler, inspector! If your proposed readership is that educated, why bother with the English translation at all?'

'And so?'

'And so we parted on a slightly sour note, agreeing to mull things over, correspond and meet again when we could.'

'Your book's never going to see the light of day, at this rate!'

'I fear you may be right, inspector.'

Ten

As Wickfield was being guided back to the staircase that led down to the exit, a pretty female student came rushing up the stairs and greeted Keuffer.

'There you are, Rudi!' she exclaimed. 'I've been looking for you everywhere.'

'Anna,' Rudi replied, 'this is Detective Inspector Wickfield from Scotland Yard. He and I have been talking in Room 21.'

'Well, not exactly Scotland Yard,' Wickfield said, 'but we'll let that pass. Yes, I'm sorry if I took Rudi out of the library for a bit. We're finished now.'

'Not trouble, I hope?' Anna asked.

'No, no,' Rudi assured her, 'just a few questions about a former student who's got himself into a spot of bother. Actually, inspector, you never did tell me what Jagger's done.'

'He's not really done anything. We're making a few inquiries, that's all.' Wickfield did not know why he was not more explicit.

'Jagger? That's the one you're writing the book with, Rudi. I hope you told the inspector about it. It's really very exciting, inspector, isn't it? It'll get Rudi his MA, and then we can get married!'

'Well, miss,' Wickfield said, smiling, 'from what I hear, the book isn't going to be finished very soon. Perhaps you should be making your wedding plans now, in case you're too old to have children when it comes out.'

'But, ' Anna protested, 'Rudi told me it was going well.'

'It is going well,' Keuffer insisted. 'Just one or two final difficulties still to be ironed out. Well, inspector,' he added, turning to Wickfield, 'it's been a pleasure speaking to you. The exit is just at the bottom, turn right. Bon voyage.'

The encounter with Anna and the short conversation that ensued left the inspector speculating. He had come away from the conversation with Rudi Keuffer with a vague doubt surfacing in his mind, and that doubt had been reinforced by the young man's comments to Anna. He decided to have a word with Keuffer's director of studies, whom he identified after a word at the secretariat desk.

'Good of you to see me,' Wickfield said, as he entered the office of Dr George Mansur, of the Political Science Faculty. Dr Mansur was diminutive and in appearance frail, but there was nothing frail in his handshake or in his demeanour. 'It's about one of your current research students,' he went on, 'Rudi Keuffer.'

'Ah, yes,' Mansur answered, 'having a little trouble with his project, I hear, but I can't think what the police have to do with it.' He looked quizzical. Without directly enlightening him, Wickfield went on to ask him to explain the research system at Windsor.

'There's a certain flexibility about our post-graduate programmes, inspector,' he explained. 'There are a number of options, depending partly on the faculty and partly on any future studies the student might wish to pursue, and each student will consult with his or her director at the start of their time with us. Now Rudi Keuffer chose a two-year MA programme with a research project outside the professors' own current concerns. A student who chooses his or her own topic has, of course, to have it authorised by the director. Now Rudi came to me with a proposed book that he was co-authoring with a former student of ours, and, having looked at the plans and the work already completed, I sanctioned it as a worthwhile MA project. I didn't know this other chap, of course - not our faculty - but his work looked good: lively and widely researched and above all innovative. I asked to see Rudi at least once a month in connection with this work, but for the rest he followed a fairly loose timetable of lectures and tutorials, undertaking various smaller essays as directed by the lecturers.'

'So what's the "trouble" with Rudi's work that you mentioned, Dr Mansur?'

'Let me explain, inspector. If the student goes in with a professor's current research, he or she is carefully guided, and specific deadlines are imposed. Less is left to the student's initiative, but there is less chance of failing to meet the basic requirements of the MA programme. A few students prefer to carry out their own work, and, as I've explained, that's fine by us, but of course more is left to the student's discretion. Now that sometimes doesn't matter. On the contrary, it's an excellent test of initiative and commitment and can guarantee a degree. In Keuffer's case, however, he was being hampered, I gathered, by his partner. According to Keuffer, his partner had no sense of urgency and moreover had a different view on the shape of the final product.'

'What did you advise Keuffer to do about it?' Wickfield asked.

'He had two options, as I saw it. Either he abandoned the joint project and began again on something new, or he persuaded his co-author to work a bit faster. You see, it was too late for Keuffer to join one of the professors' programmes. In other words, his whole MA was threatened if he couldn't get his partner – Jagger, is it? – to speed things up. Keuffer objected that the book might suffer from undue haste or lack of gravitas or any one of the other hundred defects a book can have, but I told him that I had pointed this out at the beginning of our association. His only recourse now was to salvage what he could from his present position.'

'And if he failed to produce a satisfactory work in time?'

'Then of course he isn't awarded a degree.'

'What if Keuffer had persuaded Jagger to withdraw from the joint project? Could he then have presented on his own?' Dr Mansur thought for a minute.

'Well,' he ventured cautiously, 'if we had some sort of affidavit from Jagger to the effect that he was responsible for this or that part of the work, we should have been able to judge the quality of the rest as it stood. Yes, an MA would be possible on that basis. On the other hand, no publisher would have considered a work that was incomplete.'

'Do you know Anna, Keuffer's girl-friend?'

'Yes, a little. She too is one of our former undergraduates. Why do you ask?'

'No particular reason – just wondering, really. If Keuffer failed to complete his MA, Anna seemed to suggest that she wouldn't marry him. That can't be right, can it?'

'No, I really can't help you there, inspector. Look, what's all this about? You're being a little mysterious, you know.'

'The gist of it is that Jagger was found dead in bed earlier this week; his throat had been cut.'

'Good heavens! No one would choose that as a method of suicide. You're saying it was murder?'

'Yes, I'm afraid I am. Someone badly wanted Jagger out of the way. His death would leave the way open to Keuffer's degree, wouldn't it?'

'That's a pretty drastic suggestion, inspector. Have you the slightest proof that he was involved?'

'None,' Wickfield admitted. 'He'd have had to fly over to London, and there would be some record of his flights. He has admitted that he flew over to see Jagger in February, but that can't have anything to do with the matter. I shall need to investigate. In the meantime, Doctor, thank you for your time.'

Here was a pretty kettle of fish. A prima facie case could be made against Keuffer on the basis of motive, but motive alone was never going to persuade a jury of his guilt. To travel from Windsor to Mincliffe, Keuffer would need to undertake an 8-hour flight to London, a connecting bus to Euston or Paddington, a 2-3 hour train to Worcester, a bus to Evesham – and then? A taxi or Shanks's pony, Wickfield supposed. With all the vagaries of public travel, principally time spent waiting for a connection, but also the timetables of the likely airlines, taken into consideration, he calculated that a minimum of three days would be required for a return journey from Detroit to Mincliffe. The traveller would leave a trail that could be easily exposed. Of course, Keuffer could gamble that his movements would never be investigated, but the penalties for murder were such that he might not have thought the risk worth it. Wickfield would try other checks: Keuffer's movements, passport stamps and UK border control.

With this in mind, he decided to request another interview with Keuffer. This time, running him to ground was less easy, since he was no longer in the library and the secretariat had no information. There are seven cafeterias and restaurants on campus: there was no hope of tracing Keuffer there, even though it was lunch-time. However, the student was due to attend a lecture on the political economy of international trade that afternoon, and Wickfield waited for him outside the lecture-theatre. He looked surprised to see the inspector but made no objection to being taken aside for a quiet word.

'Look, Mr Keuffer,' Wickfield said, 'before I go home I'd like to have an account of your movements around Tuesday. It seems silly to come all this way and then not go back to my DCI with the business tied up at the Canadian end. So can you tell me what you did and where you were on Monday and Tuesday of this week?'

'May I ask what this is about, inspector? You still haven't told me.'

'Lionel Jagger was found dead in bed on Tuesday morning, Mr Keuffer. We suspect foul play.'

'And I'm a suspect?'

'Purely as a matter of routine, yes. We need to eliminate you.'

'Well, you'll have to hang on a few minutes, inspector. I've got to think first.'

Other students were arriving at the lecture-hall, alone or in small groups, carrying books and note-pads, chatting amongst themselves, seemingly resigned to another hour at the sharp end of university studies. Keuffer had taken an A4 pad in his hand, and his biro was poised to write. After a minute or two of scribbling, he tore the top sheet off and handed it to the inspector.

'Look, inspector,' he added, 'would you excuse me? The lecture's about to begin. Happy to see you afterwards if you need me.' He turned towards the double doors and disappeared inside. Wickfield read:

Monday am 9-12 UW Library
lunch with Anna, Williams Coffee Pub
pm 2-3 Lecture on Issues in World Politics
3.30-6 UW Library
7.30-midnight men's basketball

Tuesday am 9-12 UW Library
lunch with Anna, Bru Coffee House
pm 1.30-2.30 walk with Anna to Ojibway Park
3-6 UW Library
6-midnight my room

It was more than possible that the librarian would remember Keuffer's attendance at the times stated, or the canteen staff his partaking of lunch. On the other hand, if they had no recollection of seeing him, that did not signify that he had not been there. A more promising activity, therefore, would be the basketball session on the Monday evening. If Keuffer attended, he could not have been 3500 miles away in Worcestershire. Accordingly Wickfield made his way to the Community Centre on College Avenue, stated his business and asked to speak to a member of staff who could assist him. He was asked to wait, and after a few minutes the Campus Recreation Officer emerged from an inner sanctum with his hand outstretched and a smile of welcome on his lips.

'Ray Fenton, chief inspector. Always happy to help Scotland Yard, you know!' Wickfield decided that his sudden promotion could again stand uncorrected. Did the prophet Joel not foretell that old men would dream dreams? 'What can I do for you?'

'A routine inquiry, sir. I need to satisfy myself that one of the students attended a basketball session earlier this week.'

'Hm, that sounds sinister! Who are we talking about?'

'Rudi Keuffer, a post-grad in the Political Science faculty.'

'Oh, yes, I know him: plays for U Lose. What's he supposed to have done?'

'I'd rather not say, if you don't mind, sir. He's probably as innocent as a new-born lamb.'

'Well, just let me check for you, chief inspector,' and with that he disappeared whence he had emerged and then returned thirty seconds later bearing a ledger. 'Monday, you say? Now let me see. Yes, yes, the U Losers seemed all to have been there. Apparently no problems.'

'Can you give me the name of the captain, sir – just to double-check?'

'Yes', he replied, reading off his ledger. 'Guy by the name of Pat Dyer. I think he's biology, but I'm not sure.'

Wickfield's tour of the university campus in his search for certainty was becoming tedious. First of all, he checked with the registrar that a Pat Dyer was in fact a student at the university and that he studied in the Biological Sciences Faculty. A telephone-call through to the Biology Building that the registrar was kind enough to make established that there was every likelihood that Dyer was on the premises at that moment, if the inspector cared to make his way to Sunset Avenue. The inspector did make his way to Sunset Avenue and found himself facing an enormous, four-storey building in pink and grey which he entered feeling that it might be functional – he was not in a position to assess this aspect - but that it was definitely not to his taste. Inquiries at the reception desk informed him that so many activities were in progress at that particular moment – seminars, tutorials, laboratory sessions, research projects, academic counselling, lectures – that it was impossible to say off-hand where Pat Dyer might be. What might be his best course of action, therefore? If he waited a little, the staff would be happy to narrow down his search. One or two telephone-calls within the building finally established that Pat Dyer was attending a lecture in Room 42, and that if the inspector cared to go up, no doubt someone would put him in the way of the student he sought. His search was perhaps more elaborate than his simple question required, but, since it was foolish to spoil the ship for a ha'porth o' tar, he persevered. Improvising a sign from a piece of cardboard torn off a stray box, he stood outside Room 42 holding up his placard and awaiting the student's exit. Pat Dyer had the sense and civility to answer Wickfield's mute call: a powerfully built individual who towered above most of his fellows. The inspector introduced himself, gave no details, but asked Mr Dyer to confirm that his team had been complete for the training session on Monday and that Rudi Keuffer in particular had attended. Pat Dyer was happy to confirm both as facts.

That evening Wickfield attended a free recital at the School of Music – an enterprising programme of Schubert and Schönberg lieder by an undergraduate mezzo soprano – before returning to his hotel. He wrote the following report for the DCI back in quiet Worcester:

> DI Wickfield to DCI Maxwell. Report of visit to Canada (University of Windsor), 20-22 March 1975, in connection with the inquiry into the murder of Lionel Jagger at Mincliffe School on 18 March.
>
> Having failed to uncover any motive or suspect for Jagger's murder at his present school, previous school or during his time as a member of Coventry rep, the inquiry moved to Jagger's five years as a student of Windsor University, in the Faculty of English.
>
> I flew in too late on the Thursday night to undertake any inquiries, but the whole of Friday was devoted to interviews. I began with Professor Miranda Hebbert, who had been Jagger's tutor in his time as a post-graduate. She revealed that there had been a little disturbance over a debate conducted under the aegis of her department and that it concerned principally a fellow-student called Keuffer. I interviewed Rudi Keuffer at some length and elicited from him the information that, far from hating Jagger, he was now collaborating with him in a book on political science. However, I also discovered that the book was proceeding more slowly than would satisfy the conditions of Keuffer's masters degree and that it would therefore suit him to remove Jagger from the collaboration: Keuffer would then be able to proceed at a speed better suited to his needs. It also transpired that Keuffer's girl-friend seems keen to wed no one less than a graduate with a masters.
>
> It took some time, and further interviews with Keuffer, the sports coordinator and a basketball team captain, to establish that Keuffer had been present on the university campus for at least some of the time between the hours of six and midnight on Monday of this week. He could not therefore have murdered Jagger. I have therefore eliminated a prime suspect. 'It is not what a lawyer tells me I *may* do; but what humanity, reason and justice tell me I ought to do' – Edmund Burke, sir!

He could imagine the DCI muttering to himself, 'I wish Wickfield would stick to the point,' or, 'Does Wickfield think he's conducting some kind of literary or historical seminar?'

The day after his return to British shores, Wickfield got together with Spooner to run over the latest developments.

'An interesting trip, sergeant: managed to squeeze in a couple of recitals and had an interesting insight into a Canadian university. Can't say I took to the architecture much, although some of the older stuff was OK.'

'Well, go on, sir, did you get anywhere with the inquiry?'

'Oh, that! No. Disappointing really. I was quite sure we had our man, and then it turns out he has an unassailable alibi.' He proceeded to give Spooner a detailed account of his time in Windsor.

'You see, of all our suspects so far, none has such a classic motive, if I may so phrase it, as Rudi Keuffer. Both his academic and his romantic life seem to depend on finishing his book in as short a time as possible – I'm not sure whether the deadline is this May or perhaps December if he wangles an extension – but either way he benefits considerably from Jagger's death.'

'And is he capable of cutting a man's throat, sir?'

'Hm, I suppose all of us are capable of it if pushed far enough. Keuffer didn't strike me as being a particularly angry or aggressive type - except that he plays basket-ball – but he's probably capable of it if the alternative is to lose his degree and his girl-friend in a fell swoop. Anyway, that's all irrelevant, as he can't have done it. I propose to take yet another step back in Jagger's career and have a look at his schooldays.'

Gentle and patient reader, the sight of italics in these lines has warned you that I am about to interrupt Wickfield's narrative with a comment of my own. I shall not regard it as a discourtesy if you choose to skip this paragraph. The development of the case has encouraged me to change my mind about the identity of the party responsible for Jagger's death. Wickfield would not have given us his Canadian adventures(?) in such detail if they led to nothing. I now think, therefore, that Keuffer is the murderer. The inspector thinks so too, and the remaining narrative will show how, in the manner of Inspector French, he succeeds in unravelling the student's alibi. I'm bearing in mind Wickfield's notorious incompetence: he's just very slow on the uptake. Anyone with half a brain-cell can see that Keuffer has a better motive for murder than anyone else who has so far appeared in the case and that it is therefore only a case of teasing his alibi apart. Of course, Wickfield will get there in the end, but the whole procedure is going to be drawn out and possibly rather tedious. If you still hesitate to follow me in my prediction, bear in mind that I have a longer and more intimate acquaintance with Wickfield's cerebral processes (such as they are) than you – or indeed probably than anybody else, except perhaps his long-suffering wife Beth. Be prepared, therefore, to stump up £7.99. I can also assure you that this is positively the last, final and ultimate time I shall intervene in Wickfield's tale, whatever transpires. Persevere, gentle reader!

Eleven

Before he could set in train this new thread of research, Wickfield received a telephone-call from the Mincliffe president. It expressed the hope that the inspector could see his way to popping over, as there had been a curious and worrying development he felt it duty bound to share immediately with the inspector. Wickfield was happy to oblige. The visitor to Mincliffe College emerges from the drive's arboreal canopy to front a great sweep of lawn set with fountain and flower-beds. The visitor's first impression is therefore one of dignity and tranquillity; he or she is inspired with confidence that this is indeed an establishment of study and quiet learning. The view inspired both Wickfield and Spooner with nostalgia for the days of their youth, tinged with melancholy at the thought that Mincliffe had become also a place of deadly hatred. It quickly transpired that Fr Jackson had lost a little of his habitual calm; he was, in a word, disturbed.

'Gentlemen,' he faltered, 'I'm very sorry to drag you over yet again, but I thought you ought to be brought up to date. I've no idea what it all betokens, but I fear for the school's reputation. Dear, oh, dear, this is disastrous. What on earth will the governors say? In fact I've asked the chairman of governors to step over this morning to see you. He should be here any moment.' The president's unease was so manifest that Wickfield offered to wait until the chairman of governors should appear, rather than oblige him to repeat his information. The president, accepting, disappeared to prepare a tray of refreshment. His office was a large, handsome room. Its two doors came off the corridor running along the front arm of the quadrangle. A massive desk dominated the room. There were book-cases and two sofas and other chairs. A thick carpet covered the centre of the floor, leaving the chestnut flooring exposed round the perimeter. The room had a certain restrained opulence expressive of the erudite and yet unpretentious personality of its occupant. Occasionally voices could be heard in conversation, either in the corridor outside or on the tarmac to the front of the building, as boys or staff passed by in pursuit of their academic ambitions (in the former case, if they had any).

The president reappeared bearing a tray of coffee, and shortly after him the chairman of governors was announced. Where the president was tall and thin and sported a shock of white hair, the chairman was short and (not to put too fine a point on it) fat, with a fringe of mousey hair round an otherwise bald pate. On the other hand, he exuded bonhomie, in contrast to the president's more muted scholarly benevolence. The chairman was introduced to them as Gerald Galliano, a businessman with premises in Evesham. He squeezed their hands with ready goodwill.

'I believe that Fr President has some disquieting news for us,' he said as he took a seat. 'Alan, it's over to you. What have you got for us?'

'Gerald, gentlemen, it's like this. A boy came to see me late last night. He'd been sent by his dormitory master. Boys can come to see me any time, but the normal procedure would be to go through a form-teacher or a house-master, so that if a matter can be dealt with at a less formal level, it can be. This is known in Catholic circles as the principle of subsidiarity. I'm proud to tell you that it was first formulated by a German Catholic theologian and incorporated into Leo XIII's encyclical *Rerum Novarum* of 1891. However, I'm wandering! Sorry, gentlemen, this business is turning my poor brain. You see, its implications are rather ominous. Right, let me get to the point without more ado.' He reached inside a drawer in his desk and drew out a crude doll, perhaps eight inches in height, in which some dozen pins had been stuck. One of the pins fixed a piece of paper to the doll's chest. The paper read, 'Death to Jagger'.

'How did you come by this, father?' Wickfield asked, pushing his glasses up his nose as the doll was passed to him.

'The boy who came to see me last night is called Hains, Lawrence Hains. He's in the fifth form. He found it, he tells me, in one of the lockers in the changing rooms. Thinking that he ought to do something about it immediately, he brought it to his dormitory master, Br Gallagher. Br Gallagher at once sent the boy to me.'

'I see,' commented Wickfield. 'Can we have a word with this boy?'

'Yes, of course, but I fear it's not going to help us much. What worries me is that if a pupil is convicted of having anything to do with Jagger's death, the adverse publicity could sink us.'

'No, no, father,' Wickfield said, 'no one is going to blame the college just because of a lone incident, however dramatic. In any case, we haven't got nearly that far yet. The doll could just be a prank, a piece of high spirits: it may have no bearing at all on Jagger's death. I think the first thing to do is to have a word with Hains. Where's he likely to be found?'

Consultation of the boy's timetable disclosed that he was at that moment enjoying the stimulation of a French lesson in Room 15. A messenger was sent to root him out, on the basis that murder was more important than the present subjunctive of *faire* (or perhaps it was the rules governing the position of negative particles), which could await another moment of exposition. Hains proved to be a very presentable lad of fifteen or sixteen, with the makings of a beard on his chaps and a lively look in his eye.

'Now, Hains,' the president said as he waved him into a seat, 'tell these gentlemen what you told me last night. Then you can perhaps lead us to the locker-room to see for ourselves.'

'Right, father, although there's really little to tell.' He turned the better to address the small company as a group. 'I'd mislaid a pair of pumps. They had my name on in ink, so no one was going to pinch them for good. After evening study, I went down to the changing-room to have a better look, working my way through the lockers systematically. When I got to one of the top lockers, which isn't normally used because it's a bit high up, I felt inside and pulled out a doll. I immediately took it to Br Gallagher, and that's it, really.'

'What time was this?' Wickfield asked.

'Just after nine, sir.'

'You say that the locker isn't normally used; but anyone could have access to it?'

'Yes, sir.'

'Anyone else around at the time?'

'No, sir.'

'OK,' Wickfield said, 'shall we go and have a look for ourselves now?' Hains led the four men round the quadrangle, out to the side of the college and so to the gymnasium and changing-rooms. The former was busy, as shouted commands from a stern voice testified, but the latter were empty. Hains made his way to a row of lockers stacked six high in the middle of the room and pointed to one at the top: an empty locker, the door slightly ajar, completely unilluminating. Wickfield sighed. Hains was allowed to return to class, rewarded by the detectives' voluble thanks for his initiative and public spirit, while the men returned to the president's office.

'Do you think this would work, headmaster?' Wickfield asked. 'Could we frighten the boy responsible into owning up by threatening to take the fingerprints of all senior boys? It's unlikely to be a junior boy, I'd have thought, because of the height of the locker.'

'It's worth a try. How do you want me to go about it?'

'When's the next time all the boys will be together?'

'Let me see. Today's Monday. Tomorrow morning, at assembly, then.'

'Nothing before then?'

'I tell you what, inspector: we'll get all the boys together today at the close of morning school. Will that suit?'

'That will do fine. In the intervening hour, is there any chance of a quick tour of the school? – just to satisfy our curiosity, you know.'

'Of course, of course, only too happy to oblige. You'll get a fairer picture of the place from one of the boys than you will from us, so I'll organise a suitable senior pupil straightaway. In the meantime, I have a parent to see, so I hope you'll excuse me, gentlemen. See you later.' Mr Galliano waddled off, a senior boy took the investigating team in tow, and peace descended on Mincliffe College.

Inspector Wickfield addressed the assembled school in the following terms.

'Boys,' he said, 'it will be no secret to you that we're here, Detective Sergeant Spooner and I, to investigate the murder of Mr Jagger in his house on Monday of last week. We have no reason yet to suppose that any of the boys is in any way involved, but we'd like to be sure. A little matter has come to our attention which we'd like to clear up as soon as possible. To this end, we're organising this afternoon a finger-printing session at which all boys from Upper Fourth upwards will be finger-printed. Your teachers will tell you when to come along, and there will be no exceptions, so whether you're having a private music lesson or are out on the sports field, your turn will come. Please bear with us in this. Of course, it can all be avoided if one senior pupil, who knows who he is, will tell his form-teacher or some other member of staff what we need to know: it concerns a doll with pins stuck in it. Enough said, or, in the words of our Roman ancestors, *verb. sap*. Perhaps he could come forward in the next half-hour to save a lot of disruption. Thank you for your attention, boys.'

A boy did come forward. His name was Robert Wood, and he was an upper sixth-former: tall, gangly, less than smart but clearly an intelligent and articulate young man. The president, the two detectives and he sat informally, that is, on sofas, in the headmaster's office, while the boy delivered his explanation of the sinister doll.

'It was a game, father, sirs, a stupid game. It all arose out of an RE lesson, in which Fr Duffin was talking about the significance of numbers in the Bible: you know, *three* theological virtues, *twelve* apostles, *one hundred and fifty-three* fish caught in the lake, and so on. This is going to be rather a long explanation, father. Do you want me to skip a bit?' he asked apologetically.

'No, no, just carry on.'

'Well, of course the biblical number that really interested us boys was the number of the beast, 666. Fr Duffin told us that most commentators interpreted the number as a reference to one of the Roman emperors of the first century, probably Nero, but he had another explanation. He added that it would take too long to explain in an RE lesson, especially when it wasn't of any direct interest, but his view was that 666, according to a proper application of gematric methods, meant "You shall destroy" - an ironic reference to the end of those who bore the beast's mark on their foreheads. It was apparently the fulfilment of a prophecy in the Old Testament book of Amos. Now none of us understood this, partly, of course, because we hadn't been given the explanation of how Fr Duffin arrived at that solution, but it prompted a few of us to investigate further. A bit of a rummage round the library brought to light a dictionary of the Bible which gave us the rudiments of what we were looking for.

'Gematria is apparently a method developed by the Jews to interpret the Bible. Each letter of the alphabet - twenty-two in Hebrew - was given a numerical value: aleph was 1, beth was 2, and so on. Words could then be turned into numbers, and any two words with the same numerical value were equivalent.'

'Could you give us an example?' the president asked.

'Yes, father. The numerical value of the name of the archangel Metatron – in legend the angel who prevented Abraham from sacrificing his son Isaac – is the same as that of Shaddai, a name for God. This was considered important, but I can't quite remember now how!'

'Yes, yes, please go on, Wood.'

'Well, the dictionary went on to tell us how complicated the whole thing became, with something like seventy-five different methods of calculation. Anyhow, a few of us decided to have a go, using the Roman alphabet because none of us knew the whole Hebrew alphabet. We took Mr Jagger's name, because he's popular with the sixth form. Well, "Lionel F. Jagger" and "Vivat Jagger" have the same numerical value. Then someone worked out that "Death to Jagger" is equivalent as well. Because I'd just had a poor mark for my essay on *Othello*, I made a stupid doll and stuck pins in it.'

'And how did it find its way to the changing-room?'

'I was on my way to nail the doll to a tree, when I saw Fr Bedford coming towards me in the distance. I dived into the changing-room and swiftly hid it in an unused locker, intending to retrieve it later. Unfortunately I then forgot about it, what with all the work that had piled up at the end of term. So that's the story, father. I'm so sorry to have caused such trouble.' His look was impressively penitent.

'When did all this take place?' the president asked.

'About a fortnight ago, father.'

'Can you put an exact date on it,' Wickfield asked.

'Let me think, inspector. It was a Sunday. That's it: a fortnight ago yesterday, Sunday the whatever it was.'

'Now in the light of Mr Jagger's death,' Wickfield went on, 'your doll looks rather sinister. Would you like to tell us where you were on the night of Monday to Tuesday last week? Can anyone testify that you were safely tucked up in bed all night? Nothing easier than to leave your room without being seen, I should have thought.'

'Good heavens, inspector, you can't suspect me of murdering Mr Jagger? Why on earth should I want to do that?'

'So perhaps you'd just tell the inspector whether you have an alibi, Wood,' the president said firmly.

'Father, I was in the infirmary with a high temperature, head-ache and vomiting. Matron can tell you. I felt unwell on the Sunday night, and she kept me in for three days. The doctor saw me on the Monday morning and diagnosed some infection and told me to stay in the warm for a few days. Why would I choose days when I was unwell to leave the school building at dead of night? In any case, the infirmary is on the first floor, and in an annexe, commanding the entrance, is a room with three beds in used as a dormitory for boys that can be trusted. It would be difficult to get out and in again at night without being heard by *someone*.'

'And who were the other boys who knew you were making a doll to stick pins in?' Wickfield asked.

'Do I have to say, father?' Wood looked to the president for support.

'Just tell the inspector, Wood, for heaven's sake. This is a murder inquiry: no time to be pussyfooting around!' Looking suitably crestfallen, Wood said,

'Michael Grant and Paul O'Connor.'

When the interview was over, Wickfield asked the headmaster for his assessment of Wood's story. Was Wood the sort of boy who might resort to violence?

'No, no, inspector. I've known the boy for over five years, and he's never struck me as anything but a good worker and a solid citizen. The idea of his committing murder is absurd.'

'But I suspect you were surprised to find him sticking pins into a doll and wishing death to Jagger.'

'I was, inspector, not in character at all, I should have said, but isn't here a huge gap between a prank with pins in a doll and cutting a man's throat? They don't seem to me to be on the same level at all. And where on earth would he get hold of a boning knife, as I think you told us it was?'

'There is that, of course. What about Grant and O'Connor?'

'I'd say the same. I'd stake my life on their trustworthiness.'

'The fact is, headmaster, someone has murdered Lionel Jagger, and at this stage we still can't rule anybody out. I'd hate to think a boy or a member of staff were responsible, but until we lay our hands on the culprit, we must keep all possibilities open.'

Back at the office, Wickfield suggested to Spooner that they sat down to go over the case. Wickfield cleared enough space on the desk to accommodate two mugs of tea and a plate of custard creams.

'Sock it to me, sergeant. Have we achieved anything at all so far, or is it just a long series of negatives?' Spooner poured his tea deliberately and chewed on a biscuit in silence, before solemnly, and perhaps a shade theatrically, producing his note-book from an inner pocket.

'Right, sir,' he trumpeted, 'here goes. Our first acquaintance with the case was a telephone-call on Tuesday morning of last week – a week ago today - from the headmaster of Mincliffe College – Fr President to those in the know - to say that one of the lay staff had been found dead in bed with his throat cut, in his house in the school grounds. We conducted an initial interview with the head, just to get the background to Lionel Jagger's few months as the new head of English at the school. This led us to interview three people most intimately involved in recent unpleasantness which had Jagger at its centre: one of the older members of the Institute staff who objected to what he saw as Jagger's desire to spread a spirit of mutiny; Helen Mansfield, his late fiancée who had thrown him over a few days before; and Jed Matthews, the game warden who had reappeared from nowhere and taken Helen off

Jagger. Br Ellison said there was no need for murder: Jagger could have been legally ejected from the school at the end of the year, if not before. Helen Matthews did not seem the murdering type – if that makes sense: what really had she to gain by murdering Jagger? and she would have had everything to lose if found out. Jed Matthews claimed to have been in bed all night: sleepless, but in bed, sixteen miles away. To prove that the hairs found on Jagger's counterpane couldn't be his wouldn't demonstrate beyond a peradventure that Matthews hadn't been in his room. Because none of this seemed very promising, we chased up Jagger's referees in Coventry: his former parish priest, Fr Croker, and a certain Mark Crudson, who seemingly doesn't exist. Fr Croker knew of no one who would wish harm on Jagger. We also interviewed the head of Ullathorne School and were treated to a digest of Jagger's theologico-political theories, but other than the delation by an unknown member of staff, nothing relevant was uncovered. We moved on to the Belgrade Theatre, where Jagger had spent three years in rep prior to taking up his first teaching post. The director was kind enough to take us through a singularly unpleasant sequence of events – unpleasant for a small, enclosed community like theirs, I mean - with Jagger intervening at the last minute, which led to the resignation of two members of the company, but nothing there looked like a crucible for murder. We got sworn statements from the then director of the company, McKinnon, and the two members of the cast who fell out over Nikki Clarke: Prendergast and Rider. Deciding to delve further into Jagger's murky past – '

'Sergeant!' Wickfield coughed warningly.

'Sorry, sir: deciding to delve further into the victim's past, Inspector Wickfield travelled to Canada to see what he could discover at Jagger's old university. Only one serious incident came to light, at which another student, Keuffer, publicly challenged him to post in the student magazine an apology for a perceived slur on his character. When investigated, this incident turned out to be less serious than the inspector had been led to understand. In fact, the two men were now collaborating in a work of political theory. In any case, the other student could not have been in Britain at the time of Jagger's death.

'Finally, we come across a little cabal in the Mincliffe sixth-form, consisting, it seems, of three callow youths – '

'Sergeant!'

'Sorry, sir: slipped out - three youths whose total motivation would fit on to the top of a wine-cork. No real and solid intent to commit murder came forth.'

'"Came forth?" Heavens. Thank you, sergeant: an admirable summing up. Where's all our investigation got us? Just line up the suspects, will you, giving them marks out of ten for probability. The murderer's out there somewhere, if only we knew where!'

'OK, sir, our suspects. The trouble is, sir, the most likely candidate, Keuffer, has a solid alibi: do I count him in or not?'

'Yes, count him in: count them all in.'

'No.1, Br Ellison, self-professed enemy of all Jagger stood for: "a conceited little pup", in his own words; on the spot; quite able-bodied enough to commit murder, but with probably little incentive to do so; worried for the future health of the college: 3/10.

'No.2, Jed Matthews, Jagger's rival in love; had been threatened by Jagger; afraid of later trouble; a half-baked alibi: 5/10.

'No.3, Dirk Rider, member of the Belgrade cast, deprived by Jagger of the love of his life - except that there are plenty more fish in the sea, in his own memorable words; plays down the effect Nikki's departure made on him; claims no more than disdain for Jagger: 1/10.

'No.4, Malcolm Prendergast, another member of the Belgrade cast; claims not to have cared very much about Jagger's interference between Rider and Nikki, so revenge not really a motive: 1/10.

'No.5, Rudi Keuffer, publicly accused by Jagger of homosexuality, if only by innuendo; despite collaboration with Jagger in a book, now, by supposition, hated Jagger because he was destroying his chances of a degree and of an engagement with the love of his life; unassailable alibi: 7/10.

'No.6, Robert Wood, all of seventeen years of age, or perhaps eighteen; his only grudge against Jagger was a low essay mark; on the other hand, could be urged on by a clique of voodoo plotters to prove himself; on the spot; weak alibi: 2/10. And that's it, sir: a very meagre harvest, I'm afraid, after a week's hard work.'

'Right, I'll tell you what we're going to do, sergeant,' Wickfield answered. 'We're going to go back to Jagger's last couple of years as a pupil at school, and if that leads to nothing, we're going to apply for Keuffer's arrest and hope to break his alibi down. I don't see what other choice we have. We've messed around for long enough, and the DCI will be getting jumpy.'

Twelve

They knew from his *curriculum vitae* that Jagger had spent the six years 1958-1964 at Norwich School. This, they discovered, was an independent boys' school situated in the close but not attached to the cathedral in the way that some similar schools are. Wickfield asked Spooner to make an appointment, so that somebody might be on hand who remembered the boy. He did this with slight misgiving, aware that he was clutching at straws: if nothing in Jagger's adult life had (as it appeared) triggered his murder, it was unlikely that dipping into his adolescence would improve the picture. Circumstances, however, forced him to do so. Spooner returned to the inspector's office looking puzzled.

'Well, I phoned the school, sir, and got a very helpful secretary. She asked me to hang on for a moment, to check that our request could be satisfied, and she came back with the information that no boy called Jagger had ever attended the school. I asked her to double-check, which she did; same result. So what do we do now, sir?'

'There are two possible explanations, sergeant, or so it seems to me. Either he attended that school, as he put down on his cv, but under another name, or he attended some other place of learning. This is very tiresome. Both alternatives seem equally likely in theory: how many employers are going to check on the candidate's school? Very few, perhaps none at all. It therefore follows that one can put down virtually any plausible information one likes. "I attended this or that school, came away with these qualifications, achieved this and that," and nobody's going to be any the wiser. However, I'm inclined to believe he *did* attend the school, particularly as for us the alternative is unpalatable: where on earth would we start looking? In any case, it's obvious that Jagger has benefited from an unusually thorough, or at least stimulating, education. Let's hope I'm right. So get back to the school, sergeant, and tell them we shall be there by midday or thereabouts, and inform the local bobbies of our impending infiltration.'

As soon as Spooner had arranged with Miss Mansfield to collect a couple of photographs of Jagger on their way across country, the two set off on their 150-mile journey to the city that, in the words of one source, was 'steeped in atmosphere and peppered with unique architectural treasures'. The rather tedious journey took them through Northampton and Peterborough, but they eventually arrived at Norwich School and were uplifted by the surroundings. The eleventh-century foundation has endured a series of vicissitudes, not least a major upheaval at the time of the Reformation, when it was separated from the cathedral and placed under the control of the mayor and aldermen of the city, and it bears the proud marks of a long and interesting history. Wickfield and Spooner had no leisure to imbibe those marks. They were courteously greeted by the headmaster, a Mr Thierry Warburton-Jones, who insisted they stayed to lunch, and they were taken to his study for the initial conference. Already present was an older man who was introduced as Dr Martin Reynolds, the deputy head. Spooner produced the photographs of Jagger and invited the men to deduct eleven years and to imagine the result as a sixth-former in 1963 and 1964.

'I've been here only seven years,' Mr Warburton-Jones explained, 'but Martin has been around for as long as anybody can remember, and he has a good memory for faces. Do you recognise him, Martin?'

'Oh, yes, unmistakeable: that's Reg Hutton. Played brilliantly for the first XI. What sort of trouble has he got himself into, inspector?'

'Now, Dr Reynolds, before we proceed, I want to be absolutely sure that this is the boy you named. There's no possibility of mistake, I suppose?'

'None, inspector. I have particular cause to remember him because of the scrape he got into in his last year. We had to ask him to leave, you know, although we let him sit his exams. In any case, other members of staff will remember him.'

'This looks promising,' Wickfield commented. 'You see, this boy, whom *we* know as Lionel Jagger, has got himself murdered in Worcestershire, where he was head of English at a boys' school. After a week of inquiry, we're really no further forward in fingering the perpetrator. He was well-liked most of the time – he upset a few people here and there, but don't we all? – good at his job, liked by the boys, did well at university in Canada, and so on. So anything you can help us with will be welcome. What's the story behind his expulsion?'

'It's quite a long story, inspector. Should it wait until after lunch?'

'That's all right by us,' Wickfield took it on himself to say. 'We could do with some sustenance!'

The party reconvened after lunch in the headmaster's study, and this is the story as told by Dr Reynolds.

'Hutton came to us at the age of twelve from some preparatory school – can't remember offhand which – and proved himself an able pupil. His parents lived somewhere inland: Thetford, I think, and the boy was a boarder in School House for the length of his stay with us. Now his best friend was a lad called Crudson, and between them they got up to a fair amount of mischief. Let me give you some examples. One morning, the domestic staff, arriving for work at seven o'clock, were surprised to find the main gate taped across with a large placard declaring that the school was closed until further notice because of the plague. On another occasion, an advertisement was placed on a local hoarding advertising the school for sale: "Town house, centrally situated, sixty bedrooms, forty reception-rooms, private chapel, no mod cons, yours for £1": I forget its exact wording, but you get the idea. Then there was the time they ran a washing-line of underpants and jock-straps from the school to the cathedral. Each time they were warned by the head that their place at the school was at risk, but each time the prank seemed so trivial in the grand scheme of things that no drastic action was ever taken. The boys' academic and sporting record saved them from expulsion, I suppose. In any case, high spirits, when there is no malice in them, are to be welcomed.

'However, they went too far in the upper sixth. There was a lad called Compton, who rumour had it was queer, although I think that in fact he probably wasn't. Hutton and Crudson decided to play a little trick on him, but the idea was mainly Hutton's. To explain this properly, I have to go back to a one-act opera called *Tamar*, written by the school's music teacher at the turn of the century, and to understand *that* you have to go back to the Old Testament. Sorry, this is beginning to sound a little complicated! Now in the Old Testament, the book of *Genesis*, the story of Tamar goes like this. Judah, one of the twelve patriarch sons of Jacob, has three sons, Er, Onan and Shela. Er marries a girl called Tamar. Well, Er dies, and Judah orders Onan to raise sons by Er's widow, but he refuses because he doesn't want the responsibility of them. Shelah isn't yet old enough to oblige. Time passes, and Judah himself is widowed. He forgets about giving Shelah to Tamar, and so Tamar isn't going to get any children. Now one day Tamar learns that Judah is on his way to Timnah to see to the shearing of his sheep, so she waylays him at the roadside, pretending to be a prostitute, and he falls for the ruse. As earnest of future payment (a young goat), she takes off him his seal and his staff. She becomes pregnant, and three months later, when Judah hears of it, he threatens to have her put to death for prostitution. She produces his seal and staff, and Judah confesses that he had failed in his duty of giving her Shelah.

'Now this somewhat sordid story was purified of its sexual content and set to music in 1909 by our head of music, Christopher Bulmer, to a libretto by Othniel Parker, who was our head of English. They called it *Tamar*, but it was transformed into a metaphor for women's right to suffrage. In the opera, Jonas has three sons, Eric, Oli and Steven. Eric marries Tamar and dies without supporting her suffragette case. Oli has no interest either. Therefore Tamar, knowing that Steven is too young to care, dresses up as an older woman and pretends to Jonas that marriage with her will bring his youth back. He falls for it and proposes. Only then, when she's got the engagement ring, does she reveal that she's his daughter-in-law. Jonas, mortified, acknowledges his fault and persuades Steven to fight for women's suffrage, as he, Jonas, should have done before. So you see the story is well bowdlerised and given an overt moral twist: Tamar feels justified in resorting to deception to obtain her right, and the opera justifies her.

'In 1964, Hutton's last year, our head of music found this opera in his cupboard and half-suggested that four or five boys could stage it. The score was a piano reduction, well within the capabilities of some of the boys. Well, the libretto acknowledged that the story was based on Genesis 38, and Hutton and Crudson found *that* much more interesting than a fifty-year-old opera, as you would expect boys to. Hutton latched on to the story to play a prank on this Compton boy: all very juvenile. Crudson had come to know a girl in the town, all of eighteen years old, who served in one of the cafés. She was known to be a little - shall we say? - forward, and Hutton persuaded her to join in his scheme. The boys introduced her into the college one night and slipped her into Compton's room. Quite what happened in the room I don't know – I doubt if anyone does, except the two involved – but Hutton photographed the girl coming out. Compton was furious, and his parents – both lawyers - kicked up such a row, rightly, in my opinion, that Hutton was asked to leave the school.

'The sequel was this. Hutton was allowed back into school to sit his "A"-levels, and he and Compton met in the corridor. Compton, still smarting under his humiliation and uttering blood-curdling threats, made a dive at Hutton, and the two were separated only by the timely arrival of two members of staff. Thereafter Hutton was introduced into the examination-room by the back door, so to speak, and there was no more trouble. Hutton, clearly seeing where the better part of valour lay, applied to a foreign university, and the school were obliging enough to submit their letter of approbation and his examination grades in a false name, with a declaration to that effect to the university. My guess is that Hutton planned to disappear, for a few years anyway, to make pursuit more difficult, if not impossible. I've had no news of him until today, and that makes sad hearing. His father went bust at about the same time as he left school, I seem to remember, which must have made his circumstances even more difficult.'

'Thank you, doctor, that's most illuminating,' Wickfield said. 'I've no wish to make unsubstantiated accusations, but this lad Compton seems to have as much a motive for murder as anybody else we've come across in the inquiry. So I think we shall have to have a word with him. Any idea where he is now?' The headmaster answered his question:

'I'll see whether the secretary can come up with an address for you, inspector. It's quite possible we've got something.' He returned to his study a few minutes later. 'The last address we have for him, inspector, is his parents' place in King's Lynn. You might care to try there.'

With help from the Norwich and King's Lynn constabularies, Wickfield and Spooner ascertained that Radley Compton practised as a lawyer in the Norfolk seaside town of Cromer, junior partner in the firm of Hale & Hayle. A telephone-call established that Mr Compton could receive the detectives at the firm's office in Cromer and would be happy to assist them in any way possible. They arrived in the early afternoon and were greeted by a sun-tanned and jovial young man, with a tall forehead, a fine Roman nose, a neat moustache and a face expressive of nothing more sinister than gentleness. He wore a bespoke suit in green tweed, with a plain white shirt and a multicoloured (browns, greens, yellows), slightly garish tie. He stood six feet tall.

'Gentlemen,' he said, as he advanced to meet them in reception, 'we're always happy to help the forces of law and order. Come on up, and we can chat more comfortably.' He preceded them up the elegant stairs and showed them into a comfortable office overlooking the street, from which the noise of Cromer citizens going about their business wafted up. When they were all seated, he asked what he could do for them. Spooner introduced the purpose of their visit.

'It's like this, sir. We're investigating the recent death of a Mr Lionel Jagger at a school in rural Worcestershire, where he was head of English.' Compton showed no emotion. 'Now we understand from the deputy-headmaster at Norwich School that you knew Jagger in your time at school as Reg Hutton. Is that correct?' At the mention of the name, the lawyer had visibly stiffened.

'Yes,' he muttered, 'I knew a Reg Hutton: a first-class ass! But dead?'

'Unfortunately, yes, sir, quite suddenly. Now we are also given to understand that there was some unpleasantness between you and him in your last term at school together. We wonder whether you could give us your version of what happened.'

'Sergeant, this is all so old: it happened years ago. What possible relevance could it have now?'

'The thing is, sir, we're trying to build up as complete a picture as possible of Jagger the man – or Hutton the man to you – so that we can begin to understand why someone should wish him harm.'

'I hope you're not including me in that last phrase, sergeant, because it's an impertinence if you are. It's true I have no very pleasant memories of the man – on the contrary I detested him – but that's a long way from bringing about his death, if that's what you're implying.'

'No one's mentioned bringing about his death, sir, so I don't know why you bring the subject up.'

'It's obvious, sergeant: I can put two and two together as well as the next person.'

'Humour us, sir: we have good reasons for asking you for an account of the incident, and we can only apologise that it should be necessary to rake over old matters, possibly better forgotten. Now, sir, perhaps you'd give us your version of the events leading up to Hutton's expulsion from the school.'

'Soon done, sergeant. One night Hutton, and possibly his sidekick Crudson, persuaded a girl from the town to come into my room. I soon sent her packing, but they took a photo of her leaving my room and were going to use it to make mischief for me. I immediately told my parents, and they had little trouble in persuading the school to expel him. That's it. That's the whole business. Sordid, stupid, but not the stuff of history.'

'But you attacked him in the corridor a few weeks later, when he came in to sit his exams.'

'Yes, but wouldn't you have done? It was the first time I'd seen him since the incident, and I saw red: silly twerp.'

'Did you intend to do him serious harm, sir?'

'How do I know? I just wanted to land a couple of punches on his ugly face: that would probably have done me.'

'OK, sir, let's come to last week. Could you give us an account of your movements last Monday and Tuesday?'

'I was away for a few days, on business.'

'We shall need you to be more specific than that, Mr Compton. Where were you exactly on the night of Monday 17 March?'

'This is an intrusion on my privacy, sergeant! I'm a married man, a respected solicitor in this town, and I do *not* wish my movements to be common knowledge.'

'They're not going to be common knowledge, as you put it, unless charges are later preferred, and I sincerely hope it won't ever come to that. So, sir, where were you exactly on the night of Monday last?'

'Look, gentlemen, I can't see it's any of your business, but I'm going to tell you, just to get you off my back. I trust it will go no further than these four walls.' He looked hard at both men. 'I was with a lady-friend in Norwich.'

'And her name and address, sir, so that we can eliminate you immediately from our inquiries?'

'Look, this is preposterous. I tell you I was engaged that night: isn't a solicitor's word good enough for you?' Wickfield intervened at this point.

'Mr Compton,' he said, 'you'll appreciate that we have to give an account to our superiors of the conduct of this case. We should be hounded out of the force if we failed to follow up a crucial alibi, so please be more cooperative. You can rely absolutely on our discretion.' The lawyer gave in with ill-grace.

'Her name is Maxine Fletcher, and this is her address.' He scribbled on a scrap of paper and passed it over to Inspector Wickfield. 'So you see,' he added, 'I couldn't have been party to any murder,' as his face took on just the hint of a sneer.

'Thank you, sir. I think we have no need to trouble you further.' They rose as a man and made for the door, glad to leave the outraged solicitor behind.

'I suppose we've got to look this woman up, sir?' Spooner ventured. 'We couldn't just take Compton's word for it?'

'No, that wouldn't do at all, not in the light of my last comments. So, it's back to Norwich for a quick call on Miss or Mrs Fletcher, and then home for us, my lad, after a frustrating day.'

Miss Fletcher, however, proved rather more interesting than Wickfield had supposed. She lived in a terraced house in Anchor Street, in the north-eastern suburbs of the city, and she was at home, preparing for herself a pot of tea and a slice of cake. A shih-tzu and a Turkish angora cat sat on the sofa, the former indignant at the detectives' visit, the latter unmoved. There was no doubt that Maxine Fletcher was a man's lady: voluptuous and assertively attractive, with clothes that showed off her figure, full lips, a skin as smooth as summer cherries, and a mop of thick, cinnaberry hair hanging in ringlets: a veritable siren. Wickfield put her at mid- to late twenties. She offered a share of her pot of tea, and both men accepted.

'Miss Fletcher – ' Spooner began.

'It's Maxine, sergeant. That's my business name as well,' and she smiled disarmingly.

'Maxine, then, we need just one piece of information from you, if you would. Could you confirm, in all confidence, that Radley Compton, the Cromer solicitor, spent last Monday night with you – not yesterday, Monday of *last* week?'

'Ooh, what's he been up to, then? The naughty man!'

'We don't think he's been "up to" anything, as you put it, but we just want to make sure.'

'Well, yes, of course he was here.'

'What time did he arrive?'

'Ooh, about eight o'clock, I suppose. We had supper, watched a film on the telly and then went to bed. Nothing out of the ordinary.'

'How can you be sure it was Monday?'

'Because I remember my clients, sergeant. That's part of my business. In any case, I've known Radley for years, ever since I was planted in his sixth-form room: what a lark that was!'

'That was you, was it?' exclaimed Wickfield, in inexplicable disbelief.

'So you've heard the story? Yes, what fun we had that night. It was his first time, you see, and was the boy shy! But we've been friends ever since.'

'So you knew Hutton as well?'

'Oh, yes, and quite a few of the other boys.'

'But, Maxine,' Spooner objected, 'Compton told us that nothing happened that night.'

'Well, he would, wouldn't he? His parents would strongly have disapproved, for one thing; and for another, he'd want to give the school authorities the impression that he was the innocent victim of a jape: his moral high ground would have disappeared if they'd found out the sordid details!'

'To go back a minute to Hutton,' Wickfield said, 'what sort of a bloke was he?'

'Reg? I liked him; I liked him a lot. He was lively and chatty, quite witty when he wanted to be, but also quite deep.'

'People have told us that there was a superficiality about him, that his learning was broad but not deep. So you wouldn't go along with that?'

'No, not sure I would. Mind you, I wasn't nearly clever enough to follow him in most of what he said, but I got the impression he thought very deeply, even though his manner was perhaps a little light-hearted. There was a serious side to Reg, you know, inspector: he wasn't just slick and learned quotations.'

'If you knew Hutton, did you also know Crudson?'

'Oh, yes, nice bloke. Quite different from Hutton, although they always hung out together.'

'Any idea what's become of him?'

'Yeah, down south somewhere: Stratford-on-Avon, I think. Works for an international debt-collecting agency. In fact, I thinks he owns the agency. He's often this way, because his parents still live round here.'

As the detectives drove back to Worcester, Wickfield ruminated out loud.

'You know, young sergeant,' he said, 'that wasn't much of an alibi our Maxine gave Radley Compton. When you asked her how she could be so sure that it was the Monday of last week, she told you it was because she knew him well: but that's not a logical answer, is it? I mean, if you asked me what I had for Sunday lunch, and I said, "Roast lamb", and you asked me how I could be so sure, and I said, "Because I like roast lamb", you'd think something was fishy – so to speak - wouldn't you? You'd expect an answer like, "We always have roast lamb on Sundays", or, "Beth spilt the mint sauce everywhere, that's why I remember".

'No, but she also told us that part of her job was keeping tabs on her clients.'

'Yes, I suppose so. But we still may have to dig a little deeper into Mr Lawyer Compton's movements that night; but in the meantime I have a curious feeling in my gut that this Crudson can help out. We've come across him only twice – once as one of Jagger's referees for the Mincliffe job, and once as Jagger's sidekick in pranks at Norwich School – but both times he's been close to the action, so to speak. The fact that he gave a false address in Coventry puts him in a somewhat dubious light – and we picked that up only because we're so good at our job!' He smirked as he pushed his spectacles up the bridge of his enormous nose.

Thirteen

Wickfield and Spooner caught up with Mark Crudson eventually at his office in the late morning of the following day. A flurry of telephone-calls established that he did indeed run a business in international debt collection, but at Banbury, not at Stratford-on-Avon. His premises were a single room in Church Passage, off the High Street, occupied by himself and two secretaries/assistants. Crudson was a well-set-up individual, exuding prosperity and self-assurance – a far cry from his pupil days, if reports were to be believed, when he navigated in Jagger's wake. This man would not play second fiddle to anyone. His wavy, chestnut hair was parted down the middle, and heavy-rimmed glasses gave him an owlish look. A smart blue suit completed the picture of the affluent businessman. Since there was no privacy in the office, Crudson suggested they moved to a café, and a few minutes later the three men were ensconced in the Chatter Box, a few doors down from the businessman's premises. Again the inspector was reluctant to mention the real purpose of their interview, on the basis, he supposed, that it would be suspicious if the interviewee betrayed knowledge of the murder. In the present case, however, it was more than possible that Crudson had read it in the papers anyway.

Wickfield explained that they had been put on to him after a visit to Norwich School and began by asking him to what extent he had kept up with Jagger since their school-days.

'Briefly, it was like this, inspector. Hutton, as I knew him then, took off to Canada for a five-year stint at Windsor. The head will obviously have told you the story of how he was suspended *sine die* in his last year. I, on the other hand, went off to the University of Kent, which was then in its infancy, to study French. Why French? No idea, really, beyond liking the language and wanting to take it further. I had no idea of employment after university; I thought I'd let that take care of itself when the time came. So while Jagger, as I had learnt to call him, acted his way through five years in Canada, I alternated between Canterbury and France for three years, imbibing the language and culture of our Gallic friends: a bit of cinema, a lot of theatre, poetry and novels, a lot of history and endless blooming grammar. Did you know, inspector, that three words are masculine in the singular and feminine in the plural? How's one expected to remember that sort of thing? And then there's the pronunciation. Apart from impossible vowel-sounds and guttural r's, some French people pronounce the s in *tandis que*, others don't; or the last letter in *but;* or the f in *cerf*. And so on. Hopelessly complex, and all quite unnecessary. I mean, if the French can't agree on how their language should be pronounced, what hope is there for the foreigner? The *Académie* do their best to maintain the language's purity – which is nonsense in itself – but it won't hold up the march of English indefinitely. However, I digress. As I was saying, Jagger and I were at different universities, reading different subjects, and there was inevitably some weakening of intimacy. However, at holiday times, when they coincided, we'd generally meet up for time together: a match, a few jars, a fishing trip, that sort of thing. In a way, our friendship improved because it matured; it became less day-to-day and trivial.

'I remember a particular conversation one day. We were talking about the level of commitment of the ordinary church-goer. He argued that there was no such thing as a "golden age" of Christianity, when society – European society, at any rate – was vigorously and deeply christianised - and I suppose he knew more about it than I did. As usual, he marshalled an impressive array of authorities. For example, he quoted Origen and Tertullian, I remember, in the third century, who complained that vast numbers of Christians were nominal only. Two centuries later, Jagger said in his offhand, erudite way, Maximus – I think it was Maximus - bemoaned the paltry results of his efforts as bishop of Turin to raise the Christian awareness of his flock, while a younger contemporary in the diocese of Marseilles, Salvian, castigated the people's failings unmercifully. Then he suddenly switched to a new French study on the Counter-Reformation which argued that the papacy's efforts to counteract the Lutheran disaster were directed at *christianising*, not *re*-christianising, European society. He acknowledged immediately that Thomas Aquinas was against him. Thomas argued, apparently, that most people have neither the time nor the energy nor the aptitude to pursue the higher activities of life like philosophy and government, and he cites Rabbi Moses Maimonides in his support. Nothing daunted, Jagger argued that it is society's task, whether secular or ecclesiastical, to *enable* citizens to pursue the higher activities. Virtue cannot be imposed, but it can be encouraged, and given the right democratic context, it will flourish. He then gave me an extraordinary example.

'He, who regarded himself as a committed and well-informed Christian, had murdered a man for no better reason than passion for the man's wife.

That was a sign of how little christianised Jagger actually was, how little the Christian virtues of temperance and charity had bitten into his soul. Then, when he told me the story, he added that he had repented. His finer feelings had won through because of his increased understanding of the possibilities of the sacrament of confirmation. Well, it was all a bit beyond me, gentlemen, but I just wished to share with you one of the last conversations I had with Jagger.'

'So you know he's dead?'

'Oh, yes, it was in all the local papers. The sad end of an unusual man: urbane, learned, dynamic, original. I'm proud to have known him.'

'Right, sir, as you'll have guessed, we're investigating his murder. Any ideas? You seem to have known him as well as anybody did.'

'Me, inspector? Why should I know anything about his murder, for heaven's sake? It was as much a shock to me as to anyone else. If I'd known anything, I'd have gone straight to the police with it, you can be certain. No, as I say, I was less in touch with him latterly than in our adolescence, and our conversations tended to be fairly high-brow, because he was brimming over with ideas he wanted to sound out on people. So I'm afraid I can't help you.'

'May I ask why you didn't go to the police with details of Higgins' death? Wouldn't that have been the normal course of action of a dutiful citizen?'

'Possibly, and I confess that the idea did cross my mind, but what good would it have done? Prosser would have gone to prison anyway for attempted murder; there seemed no point in *two* people going to gaol for the same crime. And then who would have believed me? I had no proof. Finally, I suppose, I still regarded Jagger as a friend. He had expressed his regret, he could count on the divine forgiveness. There seemed no need for me to interfere.'

'Have you ever told anyone else about his confession?'

'No, never. It couldn't do any good, and it might do much harm.'

'Just for the record, sir, can you account for your movements on the night of Monday-Tuesday last week?'

'Well, yes, probably, if you give me a minute to gather my thoughts. I'm rather shocked you can regard me as a suspect, inspector: I was his *friend*, for goodness' sake, probably his longest-standing friend at that. Let me see, Monday night last week? At home, probably. Yes, I'm sure I was. Wasn't that the night of a Beethoven piano recital on the radio? Yes, I'm sure it was. All three Opus 10 and then the *Hammerklavier* Opus 106: quite a feast for an evening! I like to follow the music in the score: keeps my mind from wandering after an eventful day in the office!'

'Can anyone confirm this, Mr Crudson?'

'No, probably not, but then they don't need to, do they?' He smiled sweetly. 'If you insist, however, you can ask my neighbour, who will confirm that at two in the morning, I opened my window and threw a shoe at their cats who were disturbing the peace.'

'Right, one last question, sir. Why did you give a false address on your reference for Jagger last year?'

'That's easily explained, inspector. You see, I was between houses. I'd sold up in Coventry and hadn't yet purchased my house here in Banbury. My furniture was in storage for a month or so while I found somewhere, and in the meantime I was living in rather primitive temporary accommodation in Italy, where I was engaged in setting up an office. Rather than give my old address, which wouldn't have served if the school had wanted to get in touch with me, I just put down the first address that came into my head. It didn't alter the quality or sincerity of my reference one bit.'

'So, sergeant,' Wickfield said when they were driving back to Worcester, 'what think you? Are we any further forward?'

'Possibly, sir. Crudson struck me as genuine. I think he gave us a new lead in that story about Higgins' death. Wouldn't Higgins' widow want her revenge?'

'Yes, just what I was thinking, sergeant – except that she must have thought Prosser was responsible. Why on earth should she suspect Jagger?'

'Well, suppose she followed her husband out of the theatre: she could have witnessed the fight, or at least the last few seconds. She could have seen Jagger administer the final blow.'

'So why didn't she say something at the time? Too scared? No proof? Or reserving revenge for herself? I wonder.'

'But don't you think, sir, that the DCI would expect us to pursue this line of inquiry? We can't really afford *not* to interview this woman, can we?'

'No, you're right. Let's see whether we can track her down.'

Before they could make any attempt to trace Amy Higgins, however, they had a surprise visit which skewed the investigation into quite another channel. A man came into the police station on that Wednesday morning, asking to see Inspector Wickfield. When told that the inspector and his sergeant were temporarily absent, he announced that he would get himself some refreshment and return at lunchtime; only one of those two men would do. When the detectives returned, therefore, from their visit to Mr Crudson, they found waiting for them a tall, thin man in his early thirties, clean-shaven, with a firm chin, a steady gaze and an honest face.

'Is there anywhere we can talk in private, inspector?' he asked.

'Of course, sir, come with us,' Wickfield invited, as he led him through to the least objectionable of the interview rooms. 'Now, sir, what can we do for you? We understand you asked to see us in particular.'

'Yes, inspector. It's to do with the death of Lionel Jagger. You're the investigating officer, I read. I have some information for you.'

'Excellent! Fire away, sir. May I just ask your name?'

'Crevan Mould. I can only apologise for not contacting you before. The truth is, I heard about the murder only yesterday, from Mr Chris Hayle – you know, the solicitor in Cromer you called on yesterday.'

'Ah. It was actually Radley Compton we called to see.'

'Yes, I know, but old Mr Hayle told me about your visit, and he rang me last night. I came straight over this morning to see you.'

'Yes, sir. So what's this information you have?'

'Well, inspector, it's like this. I don't know how much you know about the Hutton family before, well, before the blow fell, but old Mr Hayle was the family solicitor in Thetford before he set up with John Hale in Cromer. The family continued to use him for all legal matters. He was competent, well-connected in the county and above all discreet.'

'Sorry to interrupt you there, Mr Mould, but may I ask what is your interest in this matter? You seem well-informed about the Huttons.'

'Yes, I am one. Lionel Jagger was my younger brother.'

'But you said your name was Mould.'

'I did. I changed my name for the same reason he did. May I go on?'

'Yes, sorry, please do, but I was getting a little confused about how you came into the picture.'

'Let me explain, then. Reg and I – my original Christian name was Naum, but I thought this was a bit conspicuous - were the only children of Edna and Latham Hutton, and we lived quiet and comfortable lives in Thetford. An interesting place, Thetford: site of Boudicca's palace, a Norman castle, a mediaeval bishopric, a Cluniac priory, birthplace of Thomas Paine – etc. A pity it's all so flat. Anyhow, I went to the local primary school and then the local secondary school – suited me fine - but by the time Reg came to be educated, money seemed a little more plentiful, and he was sent to Thetford

Grammar for his preparatory years. Wanting to stretch his wings, he asked whether he might not attend a boarding-school in Norwich, and my parents were happy to oblige, partly, I think, because it was a sign of upward mobility. You see, my father's business was quite modest – you'd have classed us as lower middle class, I suppose, on the fringes of the professional world proper – but by degrees he prospered and was anxious for us to take a higher place in society. Foolish, inspector, short-sighted and ignoble, and it was our undoing. My first memories were of a small detached house on the outskirts of the town – in Maine Street, I think it was – but by the time Reg went to Norwich, we were living in a much posher house in Croxton, just outside Thetford: quite the bee's knees. My mother began to buy smarter clothes. We entertained more. I took piano lessons at home. When I left school, I got a job at a research chemist's in Kettering, and I'm still there: senior drug metabolist - doesn't that sound grand! – but I came home often and was proud of Dad's success as I saw signs of growing confidence and affluence.

'Then the bubble burst. Just as Reg was about to leave school and go on to university, my father was had up in court for embezzlement: tens of thousands of pounds had been siphoned off from clients' funds to finance our life-style, and dozens of investors lost their life's savings. There were angry scenes in court, and Dad was lucky to escape a lynching, if people's looks were any guide. He went down for two years. While he was in prison, the house was sold to make some sort of compensation, and my mother moved into her sister's flat, but the humiliation was such that she went rapidly downhill and died before Dad left prison. She just had nothing to live for. Dad suffered an aortic aneurysm and died on the operating table; he too had never lived down the disgrace of his crimes.

'However, the people who had endured financial loss formed a group, hired a solicitor and began to campaign through the courts for greater compensation. All my parents' property and pensions were seized, but it still didn't match the sums stolen. The court ruled that Reg and I could not be sued. By that time we had both changed our names and melted into the great society that is Britain; we had effectively vanished. End of matter. Except that it wasn't. Old Mr Hale contacted me some time later to warn me that some members of the group were forming a sort of posse to hunt down me and Reg in the hope of achieving redress, by, to use Mr Hale's expression, "exerting pressure". Now I'm contacting you, inspector, for two reasons. Firstly, this may have a bearing on poor Reg's murder, I just don't know. Secondly, the man at the head of this supposed posse, who is apparently son of one of the people who lost money in Dad's scam, is thought to be working in the Worcester area as a teacher. That puts him in your patch, inspector! The father was so distressed by the turn of events that he committed suicide, leaving a widow, a son and a daughter in straightened circumstances, and the son has vowed vengeance.'

'Have you got a name?'

'Yes: Ralph Maginniss. Teaches PE, I think. The family was from Thetford. And that's really it. I don't want you to suppose that I'm making any accusations, inspector, but as soon as I heard of Reg's murder, I knew you had to be told about all this. With the change of name and everything, you might never have found out otherwise.'

'You're quite right, Mr Mould. We're very grateful to you. We've been following a number of promising leads, but this might be just the one that proves successful.'

'Well,' Wickfield harrumphed to his junior when their informant had gone, 'this more or less wraps it up for us, don't you think? After all our investigation, the winning card is handed to us by someone whose existence we'd never suspected before! Well, it doesn't matter where the information comes from, we still get the credit. Do you remember opening lines of the reclusive Ralph Hodgson's *Reason has Moons*?

Reason has moons [it goes], but moons not hers
Lie mirror'd on her sea,
Confounding her astronomers,
But, O! delighting me.

So, the solution is handed to us on a plate, and we reap the fame. Not bad for a weeks' work.'

'Excuse me, sir, but aren't you just a little premature?'

'Not at all: all wrapped up, my lad!'

'But we haven't even found this Maginniss chap: he could be in any one of hundreds of schools in Worcester. Mind you, the County Council must know where he is. Shall I give them a buzz, sir?'

'No, sergeant, you won't: they don't employ him – Mincliffe does.'

'Mincliffe?'

'Yes, yes, Spooner. Don't you remember when the president gave us an account of the infamous staff-meeting which set Jagger at loggerheads with a number of the Institute staff? He mentioned a new member of PE staff as one of those objecting to the new contract. It's obvious to me that Maginniss followed Jagger to Mincliffe, and then it was only a matter of time before an opportunity of doing away with him occurred. Maginniss would know where Jagger lived, he was on the spot and could come and go without attracting notice. He would also have had the *sang-froid* to cut a man's throat.'

'You can't know that, sir,' Spooner protested. 'We've never met the man.'

'Take my word for it, sergeant. He's our man: I have a nose for these things.'

Within minutes the men were on their way to Mincliffe, without a previous appointment, determined to take their man. On announcing their arrival, they learnt that Ralph Maginniss had just begun a PE class with one of the lower forms, and, reluctant to antagonise the college authorities, Wickfield decided to wait until the end of it. There was no reason to suspect that Maginniss had got wind of their visit and would attempt a futile escape. They therefore spent a little time, with the receptionist's acquiescence, in revisiting the staff-room, the chapel, the well-groomed grounds and in strolling meditatively round the cloister (known familiarly, they were given to understand, as the 'quad' – redolent more of seats of learning than of monastic establishments!). Eventually their man became free, and swift arrangements were made with the head of department to amalgamate his next class with another in a spot of cross-country running. The office of the PE staff seemed as suitable a venue as any for the final showdown in the case of Jagger's untimely decease. Spooner made it quite clear to Ralph Maginniss that he was now the chief suspect and that the meeting was likely to end in his arrest for murder. The suspect said nothing. He did indeed look to be beyond words, but whether with guilt or astonishment it was impossible to tell.

'It has come to our notice,' Spooner continued, 'that your father was one of those who lost money when the business of one Latham Hutton, known as LH Financial Services Ltd, went under in the spring of 1964. Is that right?'

'If you say so,' was the sullen reply.

'I do say so: we have it on good authority. You can only have been in your mid-teens, but I bet you remember it well.'

'So?'

'I put it to you, Mr Maginniss, that from that day on, you have nursed sentiments of hatred against Mr Hutton and determined to take revenge. With Mr Hutton dead, you picked on another member of the family, his younger son Reginald. You have followed him to Worcestershire, and you have taken your revenge!'

'Rot, sergeant. Where do you get all this from? Sheer fantasy. I don't even know a Reginald Hutton; never have done, to the best of my knowledge.'

'Right, let me remind you, sir. When LH Financial Services Ltd went bankrupt, you were living in Thetford. You probably knew the Huttons out at Croxton: parents and two boys, Naum and Reg. Naum went to school locally. There was a court case and a lot of bad feeling locally. You would have known that the family had to sell up when the father went to prison. Come on, Mr Maginniss, you're being deliberately obtuse!'

'Rubbish, sergeant. I accept all you say, but I swear that I've never heard of, much less seen, a Hutton from that day to this – I'm glad to say.'

'You're telling me that you didn't know Lionel Jagger's original name was Reg Hutton?'

'Of course I didn't know. How am I expected to know that? I get a good job at a private school, I move down to Evesham, I find some bloke with the name of Jagger at the same school, and I'm supposed to have murdered him. For heaven's sake, sergeant, be sensible!'

'It's too much of a coincidence for us that you and Jagger, both from Thetford, start at the same school in the same term in a different county. Sorry, sunshine, I don't buy it.'

'I don't care whether you do or not. I had absolutely nothing to do with Jagger's death, and I challenge you to prove otherwise.'

'But you didn't like Jagger?'

'No, I certainly didn't: full of stupid quotations, looking down his nose at mere PE staff; but what's that got to do with anything? I wasn't the only one who didn't like him.'

'OK, Mr Maginniss, where were you on the night of 17-18 March: Monday to Tuesday of last week?'

'In Thetford, attending my grandmother's funeral.'

'Please tell us when you left Mincliffe and when you returned.'

'My gran died on Wednesday of the week before. The funeral was scheduled for eleven o'clock on the morning of the following Tuesday. So I drove over on the previous night, to stay with my parents and see something of the family. Fr President was kind enough to give me the whole of the Tuesday off so that I could stay on for the reception afterwards. So you can ask any member of my family where I was. We stayed talking until the early hours and got up late. Break that alibi if you can, sergeant!'

'Thank you, sir,' Wickfield cut in, 'I don't think we need to detain you any longer, but we shall, of course, check up on your movements. I hope you don't mind that.' Wickfield and Spooner left Maginniss to his solitary thoughts.

Fourteen

It came as no surprise to Inspector Wickfield to be summoned to the Chief Inspector's office on the following morning. Cory Maxwell flourished a letter from the president of Mincliffe College under Wickfield's nose and invited him to ingest its contents.

> Dear Chief Inspector [he read]
>
> Although it pains me to write to you in this vein, I must protest at the lack of tact and disregard for protocol evinced by your Inspector Wickfield, who is otherwise, I hasten to add, the soul of courtesy and benevolence (and, I may add, of erudition). He arrived at the College yesterday unannounced, demanded to see a member of my staff without seeing me first, and accused him of Lionel Jagger's murder on the base of mere suspicion. Needless to say, the member of staff concerned is entirely innocent of any involvement, as simple inquiries would have disclosed.
>
> I hesitated whether to write to you at all, such is my high regard for Inspector Wickfield's many qualities, but I felt that I owed it to Mr Maginniss and to the head of the PE department to lodge a mild complaint with you.
>
> Yours sincerely
> Alan Jackson, headmaster

'Well, Wickfield, what have you to say for yourself?'

'Nothing, sir: there is no justification, and I propose to send the president and Mr Maginniss a written apology, if that meets with your approval.'

'Very well, I think that in the circumstances that will do. Tell me, though, Wickfield, how's the case going? The death of a young schoolmaster at a private school is big news locally, and the press expect to see results. Are we anywhere near a result?'

'Well, sir – '

'Yes or no, Wickfield?'

'No, sir. Not exactly near, but maybe not far.'

'Please explain: you're talking in riddles, and riddles don't sound good on the front page of the *Worcester News*.'

'It's like this, sir. We've trawled through Jagger's life in great detail in search of a motive. We've interviewed at his present school, at his previous school in Coventry, at the theatre where he worked, and at his old university in Canada. We've talked to his best friend from school, his old headmaster, his old girl-friend, his ex-fiancée and his brother. We've been to Norwich, Cromer and Banbury looking for clues. There are people out there who would like to have seen him dead, but they've all got alibis; but there's one girl we haven't caught up with yet, and that's our immediate job, sir. We've only just discovered that Jagger confesses to having murdered her husband, in somewhat peculiar circumstances, a year or two back, and we're trying to trace her now, sir.'

'Well, I'll tell you what, Wickfield. If this lead comes to nothing, I'm taking you off the case. It's obviously beyond you, and it's time somebody else had a go at cracking it. So make sure your notes are up to date, and I can ask DI Corson to take a look. Understood?'

'Yes, sir. I'm sorry we haven't solved it yet, sir, but it has been only nine days.'

'Nine days, nine hours, it's all the same to me, inspector. Why not just admit you're not up to it? No shame in that. It's obviously a particularly tricky one.' He smiled thinly, with some small show of sympathy.

Wickfield, unable to conceal his chagrin from his junior officer, gave him an account of the interview.

'Right,' he announced at length, 'let's get on to this Amy Higgins and see where that leads us. I don't know what the DCI expects. Some crimes aren't solved after months, and this one was only last week, for goodness' sake. We're not miracle-workers or fairy-godmothers with magic wands. What does he expect, the "mewling, pox-marked horn-beast"? – don't know what it means, but it's Shakespeare.'

'Never mind, sir, we may strike lucky yet. Chin up!'

'Yes, yes, you're right, sergeant. To work, then!'

It did not take Spooner long, working through the theatrical world, to locate Amy Higgins, née Fennings-Mills, at the Birmingham rep, and the two men travelled north to Birmingham that morning, eager to take their murderer, but cautious, very cautious, in their pursuit of her. They telephoned through beforehand to make an appointment to see her, saying only that it concerned a fellow thespian from her Coventry days. Now, at this point, the inspector's notes run amok, and you can palpably see him spluttering on to his manuscript paper. Amy Higgins was, apparently, the quintessence of what Wickfield considered to be beauty. First of all, he tries a brief description, which, if my knowledge of his hieroglyphics is up to it, reads thus: 'just stunning; brunette; complexion as smooth as rolled gold; olive green eyes; charcoal-brown eye-shadow and persian-red lipstick; perfect white teeth, with wonderfully pointed canines; a warm, resplendent smile, full of health, radiance and sunshine.' To justify his temporary loss of poise, he quotes George Moore: 'Faith goes out of the window when beauty comes in at the door.' He then launches into a mini-exposition of what he is arrogant enough to call a 'theology of beauty', with lengthy quotations from (again if I interpret his hieroglyphics correctly) Thomas Aquinas, Jonathan Edwards, Karl Barth and Balthasar – amongst others! - before sliding into a more specific disquisition on the relationship between beauty and truth. Gentle reader, be guided by me: we shall proceed directly with the Jagger case!

Amy Higgins was at the theatre for an early afternoon rehearsal, and she was surprised but not intimidated by their unexpected visit. The men were invited to move into one of the dressing-rooms backstage.

'We're in the middle of a rehearsal, gents,' she said, 'so I hope this isn't going to take long.' She gave a broad smile as she arched her well-tended eyebrows.

'Mrs Higgins,' Wickfield began, 'this is about the death of your husband. We'd just like to clarify one or two details, if we may.'

'My husband? That's all done and dusted, inspector: water under the bridge. It's three years now, and Prosser, who went down for it, 's long since dead. Look, I'm trying to move on, I prefer to forget it, if you don't mind.'

'We shan't keep you long, ma'am. Could you quickly tell us what you know about the fight that resulted in your husband's death? Just briefly?'

'Oh, very well, but it's only what came out in court. I didn't see anything myself. Prosser followed Ed out of the theatre one night, waited until they were clear of the city centre and then accosted him in Spon Street. Prosser admitted to being tanked up and to wearing steel-capped boots on purpose. In court he told how Ed fell, hitting his head on a doorstep. The pathologist said that the blow that killed him was an extra one, and Prosser said he couldn't remember that, but he was convicted all the same; bastard.'

'You saw none of this?'

'No, 'course I didn't. I'd stayed behind to have a drink with some of the girls. I couldn't have helped Ed anyway.'

'We need to know that you *did* stay behind, Mrs Higgins. Could you give us the names of these "girls" you had a drink with?'

'What? What is all this? You don't suspect me of having a hand in Ed's death? That's a terrible thing to say!' and she burst into tears. Looking up after a minute through tear-rimmed eyes, she said in a firm voice,

'I loved Ed, inspector: he was a real gentleman. He may be dead for three years, but I think of him every day, and I shall stay faithful to his memory. Look, you've got me all upset now. How'm I going to go on with this rehearsal?' She looked as beautiful in her weeping as she had in her smiling. Wickfield was racked with compunction at having to persist with his inquiries, but the DCI's threat - not an idle one, he knew - urged him on; he simply had to solve the case.

Wickfield's notes lapse into astringent succinctness at this point. The detectives located three of the four girls named by Amy Higgins, still at the Belgrade, and all three, independently, corroborated her story in compelling detail. They had been playing Galsworthy's *The Eldest Son*, and for some reason rehearsals had not gone well. The first performance, however, was successful and warmly applauded by an appreciative audience. The women who played the seven female characters in the play decided to crack a bottle before going home, and they had clustered in one of the dressing-rooms to toast their triumph. One thing led to another, and the seven women - 'girls', in their parlance - had gone on to the Town Wall Tavern to make a night of it. All seven had stayed together until closing-time. The anonymous telephone-call made to the police which established the *terminus ad quem* of Higgins' murder put the murder at ten o'clock at the very latest. Wickfield was bitter but at the same time relieved. He could not believe that beauty such as Amy's could be responsible for a brutal death, despite knowing full well that some of history's most notorious murderers had been famed for their handsome looks in their own time: Adelaide Bartlett, Barbara Graham -

the 'Iceberg Blonde' - Winnie Ruth Judd – the 'Trunk Murderess' - and so on. He had semi-regretfully to conclude that Amy Higgins had no hand in Jagger's death; she could have had no direct knowledge of Jagger's involvement on the fatal night of her husband's murder. If she had no direct knowledge, could she have learnt about it from Crudson? Crudson had assured Wickfield and Spooner, with some vehemence, that he had never breathed a word of Jagger's story to a third party, until the moment of the detectives' interview with him, and there seemed no reason for him to be lying on that point. The investigation was at a dead-end. There was nowhere else to go.

True to his promise, DCI Maxwell took Wickfield off the case.

'There's no point in going on with it, is there, Wickfield?' he said. 'You've admitted yourself that there's nowhere else to go. You've exhausted every possible avenue of inquiry. I think you've probably done what you can, but it's got you nowhere. So that's it. Let someone else have a go, and if he doesn't succeed, we'll just have to add the Jagger murder to our list of unsolved crimes. I'm not blaming you entirely, as your record shows you to be a conscientious and efficient officer; but that's the end of the line on this one. Take tomorrow off, and you can start again on something else after that.' Wickfield was dismissed.

I shall not dwell on his sense of despondency. No man relishes failure. However, Wickfield adds here, as part of his sombre lucubrations at this point, a less sombre story. It occurs, apparently, in a thirteenth-century manuscript by one Stephen of Bourbon, held in the National Library in Paris. The story goes that a virtuous priest, formerly companion of St Edmund, archbishop of Canterbury, hearing that the saint was dead and that miracles were reported at his tomb, travelled to the great Cistercian abbey of Pontigny in Burgundy, where the saint was buried. He had long suffered from a painful malady, and, on the basis of their long-standing friendship, begged the saint to release him from his pain. After his earnest prayer, he knew from within that he was cured. Joyfully he returned home. However, realising that temptations to sin were even more numerous and alluring than before, he began to wonder whether in fact sickness was not a better agent than good health for keeping him from temptations and for increasing his merits. He reflected that he had perhaps been over-hasty in asking the saint simply to release him from his illness. Accordingly, he returned to Pontigny. 'Worthy Saint Edmund,' he prayed, 'please accord me whichever would be more beneficial in the things that matter, health or sickness;' and at once his former illness returned. The priest gave sincere thanks to God that he had been given the means to offer fuller worship.

Wickfield's wife, the lovely, homely Beth, made a suggestion that evening as they sat over supper (pizza and chips, followed by home-made yoghurt cake).

'Look, Stan,' she consoled him, 'don't lose heart. In the case of Adrian Carrick's death last year, you found your answer when you'd got a group of girls together and got them talking informally about their late teacher. Why not try that at Mincliffe?'

'But I've been taken off the case.'

'That makes no difference. Tomorrow's the last day of term. You've been given time off. Give the head a ring. Explain that your investigation has ended at an impasse, that you've been taken off the case, and that you're extremely sorry you've not had the success you'd hoped for. Then ask him whether you can spend a few hours in school tomorrow morning, just chatting with some of the senior boys who remember Jagger particularly, and see what happens. You never know, some new angle may occur to you you hadn't thought of before; or some new fact may emerge. Of course, you'll have to do without Spooner; but it's worth a try, surely?'

'Yes, I suppose so,' he added uncertainly.

'Go on,' she encouraged, 'don't let this case get you down. You can crack it, I know you can. You owe it to Jagger to have one final go.'

'I'm not sure I do. He was a murderer himself, remember.'

'So he deserved to have his throat cut, did he? and to die unavenged? Get away with you, Stanley Wickfield. I thought better of you than that.'

It fell out, therefore, that on the following morning Detective Inspector Wickfield drove up the red-tarmacked drive of Mincliffe College, in his own car, to spend a morning chasing a will-o'-the-wisp. He reflected that there were worse places in the world in which to while away a couple of hours. In bright sunshine, he made his way between the redwoods and the native English hardwoods to stand once more in front of the Pugin façade. He stood for a moment to contemplate the cricket pitch in front of him and the running-track and the rugby pitches beyond it. He was deliberately early enough to catch the assembly in the gym before the start of the morning's activities. He considered idly that the school uniform - black shoes, grey trousers, blue blazer with the school badge in blue and white, grey shirt and house tie - would look smart if only the boys wore it properly. He could almost hear Jagger, under the influence of the same considerations, regretting the passing of Petronius with a Bentley clerihew:

Few Romans were as tony as

The elegant Petronius.

None who dressed snappier

Appeared on the Via Appia.

He was not sure that 'tony' was much of a choice of word.

After assembly, the boys departed to pack. There were no classes that morning, but a group of sixth-formers, some of them familiar to Wickfield, had more than cheerfully agreed to meet the inspector in their common-room after mid-morning break. In the meantime, with the president's permission, he wandered round the grounds, into the library, the chapel, the art rooms and other classrooms to see the pupils' work. He strolled particularly round the quad, thinking of the generations of schoolboys who had trodden its terrazzo flooring. He took refreshment in the staff-room, with which he was now quite familiar - at one time the school's chapel, with a high, hammer-beam roof and long windows and ecclesiastical air - and met again some of the staff he had had occasion to meet the previous week. News had obviously leaked out that he was no longer officially investigating the death of Lionel Jagger; but one or two random comments seemed to express sympathy with this, his final effort to identify the murderer.

Unsure of how to find his way to the sixth-form common-room by himself, Wickfield had wisely asked the president to invite one of the group of boys to meet him outside the staff-room. It was Robert Wood! He appreciated the boy's gesture, in the light of their previous brush. Wood led him down a number of corridors, up and down short flights of steps and through innumerable doors until he showed the inspector into a well-lit, spacious room looking out on to a sort of inner courtyard. A group of boys was gathered, and all rose to greet him. They offered him a cup of tea, but, having only just come from the staff break, he politely declined. They invited him to occupy an arm-chair, whilst they drew up a variety of chairs and prepared to listen to him.

'First of all,' he began, 'I appreciate your agreeing to meet me like this. I'm sure there are many, many things you'd rather be doing.'

'Not at all,' one of them answered, 'we'd only be idling round. Helping solve a murder is much more exciting.'

'Don't bank on it,' Wickfield countered. 'Fr President will have told you that our investigation has got precisely nowhere, and that another detective team has now been assigned to the case to see whether *they* can make anything of it. What I want you to do for me, if you don't mind, is just to run over what you remember about Mr Jagger – anything at all. Something somewhere may ring a bell with me. You might just hit on an idea I hadn't thought of. Do you think you could start by telling me who you are? I'm Stan Wickfield.'

'Michael Grant, inspector.'

'Paul O'Connor, sir.'

'Roger Hammersmith – but everybody calls me Slosh.'

'Robert Wood – but you know me already, inspector!'

'Jerry Zachary.'

'Bernard Richardson.'

'Ruggiero Casartelli.'

'Good. Am I right that you represent the flower of Mincliffe society? That's what Fr President told me! No, well, actually, he said you were Mr Jagger's "A"-level upper sixth group. Perhaps they're the same thing? OK, let me ask you first of all what you think made Mr Jagger a good teacher.'

'Hard to say, inspector,' Zachary said, 'we enjoyed his lessons, but we don't analyse why we did so!'

'Fair comment,' Wickfield replied. 'So let me ask the same question a different way round. Did you feel he knew his stuff?'

'Yes, absolutely,' Wood volunteered. 'He knew his literature as no other teacher we've had here, although - '

'"Although"?'

'I think he was probably better on drama than on the novel. That sounds like a criticism, but it's not meant to be. He was probably just more enthusiastic about the stage.'

'Did you feel he'd done his homework: worked up usable notes for you, made himself familiar with past papers, that sort of thing?'

'Yes, of course, inspector: he'd hardly be teaching at Mincliffe if he didn't!'

'Was he patient when you didn't get what he was saying?'

'Well, can I give you an example along those lines, inspector?' Casartelli asked. 'He was grinding on about the rhetorical devices that occur in Chaucer: you know, *diversio, occupatio, inventio, dispositio* and all that guff. Well, I said something like, "Come on, sir, have a heart, this is boring." "Look, Casartelli," he said, "no one's asking you to *remember* all these devices and their names, but if you don't even know they're *there,* how are you ever going to appreciate Chaucer?"'

'Yes, and I can give you another similar example,' added O'Connor. 'He was outlining the six basic functions of language: referential, phatic, conative and so forth - whatever the other ones are - and I yawned rather pointedly. "O'Connor," he said, "if you can't analyse language at even a rudimentary level, how do you suppose you're going to get inside it as a communicator?"'

'How did he encourage you to be original and creative, which I imagine must be part of what "A"-level English is about?'

'All very cunning inspector.' This was Hammersmith. 'He set out for us - which our previous teacher hadn't really done - how to structure an essay. I think he said it was essentially a scholastic method adapted to our feeble and pathetic brains. You start with a clear statement of the question to be discussed. You then outline both sides of the argument, dispassionately. You then state your own point of view. Well, I needn't go into the rest of it, inspector, but he went through the stages of building up a convincing argument. Then he acknowledged that such a rigid framework seemed to leave no room for initiative. "Ah, ha," he commented, "that's where you'd be wrong! The skill is in working within those guidelines to produce a little masterpiece." He then immediately produced a Wordsworth sonnet - *Upon Westminster Bridge,* it was - and a Scarlatti sonata, which he played on his ropy gramophone. "There," he said triumphantly. "If you can't master the basic forms of composition to start with, you'll never achieve the supreme mastery of a Wordsworth or a Scarlatti. Only when you've covered the basics can you proceed to go beyond them." He then set us a discursive essay, which he marked, with copious comments, in the light of his instructions. He was very thorough.' Grant spoke up at this point:

'He got us all to learn the fifty lines of Henry V's speech before the battle of Agincourt, from "What's he that wishes so?" to "That fought with us on St Crispin's day". He gave us the background to the speech, with details of the difficulties the English were labouring under and the political situation, and then encouraged us to recite all or part of it in class. His point was that there was no one way, no perfect way, of delivering the speech: each pupil was to make of it what he could and project his own personality.'

'But he'd also inject little games which kept us on our toes,' said Wood.

'Such as?' asked Wickfield.

'At the end of a dense session on literary analysis or some such, he'd write on the board a sentence like, "Do geese see God?" or, "Go hang a salami: I'm a lasagna hog", and then asked us to come up with instant reactions. We'd then have a go ourselves.'

'OK,' Wickfield said, 'it seems that Mr Jagger was the perfect teacher; but he can't have been. What *didn't* you like about him?' For a moment the room was silent. Then Wood piped up.

'One thing that's not been mentioned, inspector, if I can just go back a bit, is that he respected people's opinions. It didn't matter what your view was, provided you had a reason for it, he took it to be valid as far as it went. So: egalitarianism in action! And he once quoted Albert Einstein – I think it was Einstein – "Before God we are all equally wise – and equally foolish". But as to what I didn't like about him, he always smelt of cigars!'

'He could lose his temper when he thought we made light of war or suffering.'

'He couldn't disguise when he disliked a writer or a genre. "What are thrillers *for*?" he'd ask rhetorically. Or, "What's the point of Virginia Woolf?" "Sci-fi?" and he'd raise his eyes to heaven and sigh.'

'Did he ever show favouritism in class?'

'No, never,' said Zachary with feeling. 'He must have had his favourites – all teachers do – but he never showed it in this group. Am I right, guys?' General nods of assent.

The conversation wound to its end. All the boys spoke, all had something to say, usually adulatory, about the deceased; but Wickfield was unsure whether it had advanced his investigation. He thanked them very much and prepared to leave. Wood immediately told him that Fr President hoped he would accept an invitation to stay for lunch and that they hoped he would have lunch with them. He was impressed and grateful. The gesture went some way to relieving his tired spirits.

Fifteen

However, when his wife returned home at the end of the working day, she announced that she had taken it on herself to invite Spooner to supper and that that very evening the case of Lionel Jagger would be solved, by hook or by crook. She had invited both Spooners, but the sergeant's wife had been unable to engage a baby-sitter at such short notice and asked to be excused. Wickfield was only too glad to have Spooner as company at supper, but he greatly feared that the effort would be wasted. They had explored every avenue, they had considered every hypothesis. The result was, in Coleridge's words, 'Nothing before and nothing behind but the sky and the ocean'.

'But you see, Stan, what you haven't yet done is to go over the case as a whole, in the light of your session this morning with the sixth-form boys, using Spooner as a sounding-board. It'll work, you'll see. I have every faith in you, my darling - most of the time.' She disappeared into the kitchen, while the inspector sat moodily in the sitting-room, failing to concentrate on Milan Machoveč's *Jesus für Atheisten*, which had just arrived in the post. Spooner arrived, the three sat down to sausages, onions and mashed potato, followed by a cherry cheesecake prepared the night before by the lady of the house. There was an enforced normality. Never before had the inspector been taken off a case, and the event weighed heavily on the little party.

After supper, when the important business of the evening began, Wickfield, looking grim but determined not to let Beth down, prepared to do battle with the data.

'Now, Spooner,' he said, 'our investigation had us going backwards, necessarily. We started with Jagger at Mincliffe, then Jagger at Bishop Ullathorne, then Jagger at the Belgrade, and so forth. If you wouldn't mind, could you take us through everything in chronological order? You never know, something may strike one of us if we look at things from a slightly different perspective.' Beth placidly took up a piece of embroidery. Spooner cleared his throat, grinned and waved his notebook defiantly.

'Soon have it all in the open, sir. Here we go. Jagger was born in 1946 in the Norfolk town of Thetford, the younger son of a financial adviser and his wife. He attended the prep department of the local private grammar school before going on, at his request, to Norwich School. There he prospered, both in academic work and in sport. He and a mate of his, Mark Crudson, got up to a fair amount of mischief, and on the final occasion, the pair went too far, at Jagger's instigation. Inspired by an opera unearthed in the school music archives, which was in its turn inspired by one of the less elevating stories in the Old Testament, Jagger and Crudson persuaded a local girl to infiltrate the school and molest a sixth-former, Radley Compton, in his room. The boy's parents, who were local solicitors, kicked up such a fuss that the headmaster was obliged to expel Jagger, allowing him to return only to sit his "A"-levels.

'At the same time as all this was going on, Jagger's father's business went bust. It came out that he had misappropriated his clients' funds and beggared not a few of them. He had used the money to move to a better house in the village of Croxton, to send his younger son to Norwich School, and generally to improve his family's life style with smart clothes, foreign travel and so forth. The effect on the Jaggers was devastating. Everything went: the house, the furniture, the savings, the pension pot. Mr Jagger went to prison and died there, Mrs Jagger went to stay with a sister and died as well. Both the Jagger sons changed their names and disappeared.

'We pick up the threads of Lionel Jagger's life at Windsor University in Canada, where he had undertaken a five-year, two-degree course in English and drama, 1964-1969, under his assumed name. In the person of the inestimable Inspector Wickfield, we spent some time at Windsor, extracting information and establishing alibis. The most, the only, promising incident was a university debate in Jagger's last year which put him at odds with a student from the political science faculty. Jagger and this other student, Rudi Keuffer by name, were leaders respectively of the two sides of the debate, and Jagger made some stupid remark which cast aspersions on his opponent's sexual proclivities. There was some frank exchange in the university magazine, but in the end, after the intervention of a couple of friends, the two were reconciled and even became collaborators in a philosophico-political book to be entitled *Eutopia*. This collaboration was continuing but seemed to have reached something of a blockage at the time of Jagger's death.

'When Jagger graduated, he got a job at the Belgrade Theatre in Coventry, a repertory company, where he spent the next three years. Two incidents during his time there engaged our particular attention.' Spooner looked up from his notes, but neither the inspector nor his wife made a comment; they were concentrating hard on the life-history of a murdered man. 'The first concerned a girl called Nikki, one of the company, who had two male admirers, a man called Rider and one called Prendergast. Jagger butted in uninvited, and the result was that all three – Nikki, Rider and Prendergast – left the company, for one reason or another. Prendergast was going anyway, but Nikki was quite a loss. The other incident, which never came out in public, was when Jagger helped kill a man called Higgins after he had been attacked by a drunken admirer and former flame of his wife, Amy. Prosser – that was the assailant's name - went down for murder and died in prison. Jagger later told his old school-friend Crudson about it, as he stated to ease his conscience.

'From the theatre, Jagger moved to a secondary school in the same city, the Bishop Ullathorne Catholic school, where he taught English and drama as a junior member of the department. Mr Williams, the headmaster, told us that, after two years, he had had to invite Jagger to look for a post elsewhere, as a teacher had complained, via a governor, that Jagger was spreading heterodox opinions, not just amongst the staff, who were mostly immune to his maunderings, but, it was feared, amongst the pupils, whose powers of discernment would be much less developed. Otherwise Jagger had proved to be an exemplary teacher.

'From Bishop Ullathorne, Jagger accordingly moved to Mincliffe. His reference from his parish priest was perfectly acceptable, as was – of course! - the reference from his old companion in sin, Mark Crudson. Because of his good qualifications, his experience at Bishop Ullathorne, and his undoubted expertise in the field of drama, Jagger landed, at twenty-eight, the post of head of English. He immediately established himself as an asset to the staff: organised, well-informed, lively, popular. No school could wish for more than this! However, trouble loomed, on two fronts. First of all, he upset some members of staff, notably one of the retired brothers, by making what many considered an inopportune intervention at a staff-meeting. He had already put some backs up with scattered remarks critical of the school or the Church and with a general air of superiority. Secondly, he became engaged to a member of the science department, Helen Mansfield. On the very day of their engagement, an old flame of hers appeared from nowhere, and she cancelled her engagement with Jagger. There was a tense encounter between the two men, which ended with Jagger threatening the other man. The weekend intervened, and Monday was the last day at which Jagger appeared in school. By the Tuesday morning, he was dead.' A lengthy and considered silence fell at the end of this recital.

'Right, sergeant, keep going,' Wickfield said at last. 'Enumerate our suspects.'

'OK, sir. This is what we've got, in chronological order. The earliest, chronologically speaking, is Radley Compton, a solicitor in Cromer, Norfolk. He was the boy taken for a ride at Norwich School in his last year. He had motive, possibly – revenge nursed over a number of years – but he has an alibi for the time of Jagger's death: he spent the night, unknown to his wife, with a long-standing friend, Maxine, who turned out to be the girl who had bedded him at school. From much the same time, we have the Maginniss family, in the person of their son Ralph, who, it transpired, had landed a job at Mincliffe at the same time as Jagger. Coincidence, or what? The Maginnisses were one of the families ruined by Jagger's father's financial misdoings. Again, young Ralph had ample motive, but he too has an alibi: he was at home back in Thetford preparatory to attending his grandmother's funeral on the following day. We checked this alibi, and it held.

'From Windsor University, we picked on Rudi Keuffer as a likely suspect. His spat with Jagger was apparently healed, but no one can say how it might have festered over the intervening years. A new cause of tension was introduced by Jagger's dilatoriness in proceeding with his part of the collaborated book. This was holding up both Keuffer's degree and, seemingly, his engagement to his girl-friend. However, he had an alibi, which was checked: at the time of Jagger's death, he was in Canada, enjoying a basket-ball practice with a couple of dozen other students and a trainer; and that's taking into account the time difference. Twice three and a half thousand miles is a long way to travel in a couple of hours.

'From Jagger's time at the Belgrade, no less than three suspects emerged from the first incident: McKinnon, the theatre's manager at the time, and Rider and Prendergast, the two members of the cast whose nose Jagger put out of joint. Their sworn statements, however, revealed that real motive for murder was lacking – as we suspected in any case. From the second incident, two possibilities were canvassed and investigated: Crudson, who was the only one to be party to Jagger's contribution to Higgins' death, and the widow, Amy. Crudson's alibi was that he was at home in Banbury, listening to Beethoven and then sleeping. At two o'clock in the morning, he claimed that his neighbours heard him throw a shoe at an obstreperous cat; that claim was substantiated by our inquiries. Amy's alibi was that she was having a night out with half-a-dozen fellow-actresses, and it was confirmed.

'Moving on to Jagger's first post as a teacher, the only thread, and it's a slender one, was provided by a Mrs Marinoff, one of the governors.

However perturbed she herself was by Jagger's philosophy, the impulse to encourage Jagger to move on was provided by an unnamed member of staff. We did not pursue that, because all motive seemed to be lacking. Why go the trouble of murdering Jagger six months later, when he left the school anyway?'

'Finally, therefore, we come to Mincliffe, where the inquiry all started. Here we focussed on three individuals. Firstly, Br Ellison, and this is what we commented at the time: "self-professed enemy of all Jagger stood for: 'a conceited little pup', in his own words; on the spot; quite able-bodied enough to commit murder, but with probably little incentive to do so; worried for the future health of the college." We awarded him 3/10 on the scale of likelihood, largely because the school could have got rid of Jagger without his having to resort to violence. Secondly, Jed Matthews, Jagger's rival in love; he'd been threatened by Jagger and was perhaps afraid of later trouble, when he'd moved off with Helen to his island paradise. His alibi is OK, but it depends on something he overheard his father say at dead of night. And thirdly, Robert Wood, seventeen- or eighteen-year-old schoolboy, inmate of Mincliffe College, Worcestershire. The opportunity's there, but real motive again seems totally lacking. His alibi is that he was in the infirmary with an indisposition and would have been heard by a number of people if he had escaped in the night to murder his teacher.

'And just look at the number of people we've interviewed: dozens, or at least it feels like it! In Norfolk, we've seen Dr Reynolds (deputy head of Jagger's school), Radley Compton (the solicitor of Cromer, who was the boy Jagger played a trick on), and Maxine Fletcher (the girl at the centre of it all). At Windsor, you saw Professor Hebbert (Jagger's tutor), Rudi Keuffer (the student Jagger insulted), Dr Mansur (Keuffer's director of studies) and Ray Fenton (the Campus Recreation Officer). At the Belgrade, we interviewed or received statements from Madge (the deputy director), McKinnon (the previous director), Prendergast and Rider (the two men anxious to attract Nikki's attentions). We saw both Mr Williams (the head of Bishop Ullathorne School), and Fr Croker (Jagger's parish priest in Coventry). At Mincliffe, we have seen Frs Jackson, Bedford and Hendon (the senior management team), Br Ellison (retired English teacher, living at the college), Miss Mansfield (biology teacher), Jed Matthews (her long lost amour), Lawrence Hains (the boy who found the voodoo doll), Robert Wood (the boy who made the said doll), six other boys as a group, and Ralph Maginniss (PE teacher). Independently, we have had deep and meaningful conversations with Mark Crudson (Jagger's long-standing and long-suffering school-friend), Crevan Mould (Jagger's older brother) and Amy

Higgins (Ed Higgins' widow). I said dozens, and I think it is dozens.' He paused to count. 'Thirty-one, my friends!' he announced. 'That's about it, sir: as thorough an investigation as I have ever been part of! Thank you for the opportunity of seeing you at work once again!'

'Yes, but we haven't got our culprit, have we, young Spooner? and I'm not sure that much is stirring in my upper storey. I seem to be going round and round the same stuff time and again. While I meditate, do you think we could do with a cup of tea, Beth?' Tea came on a tray, with a plate of ginger nuts by way of a second supper, and the three sat in silence for half-an-hour. Beth embroidered; Spooner sat staring at his note-book; Wickfield shuffled through his notes. Only the mantle piece clock, the occasional slurp of tea and some rustling of papers broke the silence. It is probable that all three realised that if the current session failed to break the deadlock, the case was lost: it is unlikely that they would ever again have all the material so freshly and closely to hand. It was galling, however, to think that so much depended, not on meticulous forensic examination, on undeniable laboratory testing and results, but on an elusive idea or a connection of elusive ideas; and those could not be summoned at will from the distant recesses of the mind. Night had drawn in; the curtains were closed. Time passed and peace reigned; but it was a tense sort of peace.

'That's it!' Wickfield suddenly shouted. 'Got it! It was the chat with those seven boys this morning wot did it. Excellent, my dear,' he said, rubbing his hands together. 'You were quite right to insist I went back to Mincliffe and spoke with Jagger's English class. What foresight you have!' He beamed triumphantly, and the other two could not help but beam back.

'This calls for a small celebration, my dears,' announced Wickfield. 'What say you we have a glass of something stronger than tea?'

Sixteen

'There's only one thing I need to check,' Wickfield said, 'although I'm pretty sure I'm right.' With that he rose, went over to one of the bookshelves and took down *A Dictionary of Saints*. He leafed through it quickly, clearly found what he was looking for and sighed happily. 'Bingo!' He resumed his seat, smiling seraphically, triumph and satisfaction suffusing his craggy face.

'Well, come on, Stan, don't keep us in suspense! Who did it, and how did you rumble them?'

'As I said, it was this morning's meeting with those seven boys that nudged me in the right direction. I'd failed to spot the tiniest slip-up as we talked and listened our way through the last ten days, and it was that slip-up that revealed the murderer's identity. There always is one, isn't there? They can't avoid making a mistake somewhere along the line; but it was only what the boys were saying this morning that put me on to it.'

Even as he spoke, the telephone rang.

'I'll get it,' Beth said, 'but not another word, Stan, until I get back.' She disappeared into the hall and came back a short while later, whispering,

'It's that dolt Maxwell: they've made an arrest, and he wants to brag about the achievement – to make you feel small, I suppose. "Look here, Wickfield," she mimicked, "you've been on this case nearly a fortnight and got nowhere. Corson catches on in a matter of hours!" Leave the door open, Stan, I want to hear as much as I can!'

'Hello, chief inspector, Wickfield here ... you have? ... very good. I congratulate you! ... Yes, I'm sorry I didn't spot that ... How? ... And do the hairs match? ... Well, the force got there in the end ... Pass on my felicitations to DI Corson, will you, sir? ... Yes, and the same to you, sir ... Goodnight.'

Wickfield re-entered the sitting-room, hardly able to conceal his mirth.

'Well, have they got him, Stan?' asked Beth impatiently.

'Yes, they've arrested the culprit.'

'Who?'

'Jed Matthews.'

'Well, I never. We did consider him, sir, so we just failed to find the proof that DI Corson's found. Well, I never did,' he repeated. 'That's a turn-up for the books. What are you smiling for, sir?' Wickfield laughed, and laughed again, and then sat back in his chair, tears of amusement running down his cheeks.

'Dear, oh, dear,' he gasped at last, 'I haven't laughed so much in ages. It's such a release.'

'Right, you've had your laugh, Stan, now tell us what Maxwell said.'

'Corson apparently spent a couple of hours this morning reading through my notes. He congratulates me, by the way, on their clarity and completeness: he's more of a fool than I thought! He spotted the weakness of Matthews' alibi and telephoned the father in Worcester. The father couldn't at all remember his wife getting up in the night, and he certainly couldn't remember shouting out to her in the bathroom. Out the window goes Matthews' alibi, therefore. The rest was circumstantial. Matthews had been threatened by Jagger; he also feared that he would always have Jagger in the background, trying to get Helen away from him. His peace of mind would be gone for ever unless he could counter the threat. He therefore resolved to put Jagger out of the way once and for all. He drove over to Murcot from Worcester; his two previous visits had shown him the lie of the land. He took the elementary precautions of arming himself with a sharp knife and wearing gloves, committed the murder and then drove back to Worcester, leaving the murder-weapon behind.'

'And did the hairs found on Jagger's counterpane match, sir?'

'The DCI told me he hadn't try to match them; it was only a formality anyway, as he was absolutely certain it would be the nail in Matthews' coffin. End of case. All nicely wrapped up, and Wickfield looking like an idiot who failed to test the simplest alibi. Maxwell was reasonably philosophic about it. Body found on the Tuesday, the murderer arrested a week the following Friday – just eleven days. It didn't matter which of his officers solved the case, as long as he could announce success to the papers. Maxwell's team had done it again! Dear, oh, dear,' and he began laughing again.

'Right, Stan,' Beth said impatiently, 'get a grip and tell us what *really* happened!' The inspector gathered himself together and began the serious exposition of the case.

'Let me begin by echoing a comment young Spooner here made earlier: we seem to have covered the ground very thoroughly and interviewed widely. Now I know that in the past we've had cases where the perpetrator of murder has turned out to be someone unknown to us or only remotely connected with the main action, but I thought that unlikely here. We had delved into every section of Jagger's life, from childhood to his last job, and I was confident that, in the life of a man of only twenty-eight, the spread of our net was more than adequate. The consequence was that one of the thirty-one people enumerated by Spooner was our killer. It would be unjust to pick at random, and a waste of police time to carry on following false leads. The trouble was that all our suspects had an alibi. One of those alibis was fake: but which one? I cottoned on to which one it was when I recollected a snatch of this morning's conversation with the Mincliffe boys. They were reminiscing about Jagger's habit of keeping the class on their toes by mixing serious with less serious material, and one of them brought up a couple of palindromes: Do geese see God? and Go hang a salami: I'm a lasagna hog.

'Before I got that far, however, I'd spotted the one mistake made, not by the murderer, but by the murderer's accomplice. You'll remember, of course, Henry V's famous speech on the eve of the battle of Agincourt, in which he fired the English army to defeat the vastly superior French forces.

> He that shall live this day, and see old age,
>
> Will yearly on the vigil feast his neighbours,
>
> And say 'To-morrow is Saint Crispian.'
>
> Then will he strip his sleeve and show his scars,
>
> And say 'These wounds I had on Crispin's day.'

This speech came up this morning, when one of the boys told us how Jagger got them to memorise it and then deliver it from memory, each in his own way. Jagger's point was obviously that in art there is no one way of doing things, that the judge must exercise great discretion in ruling out performances as illegitimate or inferior. It occurred to me then that in the Jagger case we had come across another saint's day: the feast-day of St Edward the Martyr. Let me remind you of its occurrence. When we interviewed Mark Crudson in a greasy spoon just down the road from his Banbury office on Wednesday morning, Crudson reminisced about a conversation he'd had with Jagger, at some unspecified time in the recent past. "I remember a particular conversation," he told us. "We were talking about the level of commitment of the ordinary church-goer," he went on, and the continuation of his reminiscence included the tale of how Jagger had struck Higgins' head on the doorstep, and in particular the detail that Higgins died on St Edward's Day. Jagger is said to have remarked that there was a certain justice in that, because Higgins' Christian name was Edward. Now I've just checked the St Edward entry in Attwater, to confirm a vague memory of my own. There is some confusion over the saint, but the indisputable part is that he was murdered at sixteen, in 979, so that his half-brother Ethelred could mount the throne. There is debate about whether the lad was killed near Bury St Edmunds, which is the more likely option, or near Diss or rather near Norwich, and there seems little evidence to substantiate his death as a martyrdom, but what struck me about the whole story was the date: 18 March. Now Jagger died on 18 March, three years later to the day. This could not be just coincidence. Everybody knew, whether they consciously adverted to it or not, that Higgins died on 18 March, the feast of St Edward the Martyr, but only one man knew of Jagger's involvement: Crudson. Crudson's mistake was to include that detail in his version of the story of how Higgins died. If he had left it out, we should never have known the precise date on which Higgins' death occurred. We could always have found out, of course, but why should we have bothered? How could we ever have known that it was significant? The fact that Crudson drew attention to it was a sure sign that in his own mind it mattered. He would have done better to gloss over it. I think it was an oversight, and he included the date without thinking, rather than as a direct challenge to the police to make the connection.

'Once I'd focussed on Crudson as the architect of Jagger's murder, I looked more closely at his alibi. He threw a shoe at his neighbour's cats at two in the morning, after an evening of quiet listening to Beethoven piano sonatas. We checked on this alibi, and it was confirmed, even though it looked contrived: deliberately engineered to persuade us that he was in the clear. Now Banbury is forty miles from Evesham, certainly an hour's drive, given the cross-country route required, even at dead of night. There is no possibility that Crudson could have murdered Jagger at, or anywhere near, the time established by the pathologist. Of course, he could have put his neighbour up to a spot of perjury, but before I came to that conclusion, I sought an alternative. Whom else did Crudson know that had a grudge against Jagger? At least two people: Radley Compton the lawyer, who was at school with him, and Maxine Fletcher the – well, let's call her a mutual friend. He might also have met Rudi Keuffer on his visit to Jagger at half-term in February, but I ruled out a significant connection because of Keuffer's alibi.

'Compton, Fletcher and Crudson go back at least ten years, friends or at least acquaintances in adolescence if not before. Now I've twice named Compton before Maxine: the order, I realised, was significant; and this is how. We had been put on to Compton in Cromer by the deputy-head of Norwich School, Dr Reynolds, who well remembered the prank which led to Jagger's suspension or expulsion, whichever it technically was, ten years before. For his alibi, Compton told us coyly and with every appearance of truth that he had spent the night of Jagger's murder in Maxine's company in Norwich, and she confirmed this. This is where the Mincliffe boys' palindromes suddenly struck me between the eyes. A palindrome works both ways, and some of the longer ones, while perhaps being more ingenious than sensible, are at least impressive. I asked myself what we should have thought if, instead of going to Compton first, we had been pointed in the direction of Maxine. If we had interviewed Maxine first – and in the nature of the investigation, this was very unlikely – but if we had, and if we had asked her for an alibi, she'd naturally have given Compton. "Oh, officers, I had a gentleman friend/client all night: so cosy," etc. It was a story concocted by the two of them that was difficult to break. We were anxious to establish Compton's alibi; we should have been more anxious to establish Maxine's.

'From there, I wondered why Maxine should need an alibi. It was obvious: she was not where she or Compton claimed she was. For the sake of appearances, it was probable that the Cromer lawyer had spent the night at her flat; but as sure as eggs is eggs, *she* hadn't. I then wondered what could have driven this pretty, seemingly harmless girl to drive all the way across to Murcot, on St Edward's Day, missing part of the family get-together before her grandmother's funeral, to kill Jagger in cold blood. Could it be the shame of being used by Jagger in a prank on Radley Compton? That didn't seem very likely. I then remembered that the Maginniss family – you know, one of the families ruined by Hutton senior's financial fiddling in 1969 - had included a girl as well as a boy: an unnamed daughter alongside Ralph Maginniss, the PE teacher at Mincliffe. It was Jagger's older brother, Crevan Mould, who told us that. What if Maxine's "real" name was not Fletcher but Maginniss? Pure supposition on my part, but the more I thought of it, the more promising my idea came to seem. We had only Compton's and Maxine's word that she was called Fletcher; we had no reason to question it; it seemed a safe ploy.

'As I see it, then, this is how the plot worked. We haven't investigated how Compton and Crudson regarded each other, either at school or since, but Maxine was a mutual friend. I'm not sure, therefore, who sowed the seeds for the conspiracy. Perhaps Maxine and Compton got talking, determined on a way of doing Jagger in, or at least down, and then took Crudson into their confidence. Crudson provided the date for what amounted to a ritual execution: the very anniversary of Higgin's brutal murder. Jagger thought he had got away with it: but Nemesis was in the wings, not to be thwarted. They probably had to wait three years until Ralph was in place to guide his sister. Crudson could keep Maginniss - or perhaps I should now say the Maginnisses, brother and sister - informed as to which school Jagger was applying for. Probably there was no simultaneous vacancy in PE at Bishop Ullathorne, but there was at Mincliffe. Once installed, Ralph could provide all the local information: the best approach by road, where to leave the car, which house was Jagger's, other likely movements in the vicinity. Of the three, Maxine had the strongest motive: her family had been ruined. Compton smarted, all these years on, from being the butt of a silly joke that pandered to the other boys' malice. Crudson felt he had to do something to bring justice to Higgins' memory and to Amy's bereavement; it was intolerable that Jagger should boast of his action, even if he simultaneously confessed to pangs of conscience. We shall probably never know what mechanism the three conspirators used to decide on which of them should carry out the murder: lots? reading of tea-leaves? a crystal ball? or – irony, this – a democratic vote? I should like to think perhaps the latter. It could be, I suppose, that Maxine volunteered quite willingly. When the moment of execution comes, we can imagine her seizing her victim by the hair and shouting, "This is for the Maginniss family – and not forgetting Ed Higgins." He awakes; sees his Nemesis; she wields the knife pitilessly; he's caught staring in horror at his fate and knowing that his sins, and his father's, have caught up with him. While I've come to admire Jagger for his many qualities, to sympathise with him to some extent in his loss of Helen, and to bewail the loss to education in which his death has resulted, I cannot *entirely* bring myself to condemn Maxine for her act of revenge.'

I'm very sorry, dear reader: I was wrong – well, mostly. I offer my sincerest apologies, and in line with my promise, I do so willingly. I hope I didn't mislead you? I must add that I take my hat off to Wickfield for teasing apart a very clever plot. I'm sure I shouldn't have picked up the clues on my own: and then you would have been faced with the disappointing narrative of an unsolved murder! JF

Lightning Source UK Ltd.
Milton Keynes UK
11 November 2010

162705UK00001B/55/P